Going Too Fast

stories by

Lynne Viti

Finishing Line Press
Georgetown, Kentucky

Going Too Fast

ACKNOWLEDGMENTS

The author wishes to acknowledge the editors of the following publications in which the following stories first appeared:

Connections Magazine	"Tony Bennett, Aldous Huxley, and Eddie:"
Cultured Vultures	"One Night Stand, With Mittens"
Drunk Monkeys	"Take Gutman"
Indie Affair	"Good Catholics"
Moondance, The Woven Tale	"Going Too Fast," "The Real Thing"
Right Hand Pointing	"How We Got Married"
WILLA	"Peaches"

Publisher: Leah Maines
Editor: Christen Kincaid
Cover Art: Jeff Blum, *Central Park Summer*
Author Photo: Richard Howard
Cover Design: Gina Maranto
Drawings: Barbara Aronica Buck

Printed in the USA on acid-free paper.
Order online: www.finishinglinepress.com
also available on amazon.com

Author inquiries and mail orders:
Finishing Line Press
P. O. Box 1626
Georgetown, Kentucky 40324
U. S. A.

Table of Contents

For Tom, who taught me to slow down

For Sr. Augusta Reilly, RSM and Sr. Carol Wheeler, RSM,
who taught me to write

How We Got Married

Paul and I are standing on the corner of 116th and Broadway when up pulls a black late model Cadillac. Out jump Jaime and the lovely longhaired, skinny, tanned, bare-armed Boo. Her real name is Eleanor.

—Want a ride? they ask. Boo is wearing blue engineer stripe jeans and a white T-shirt, no bra, and her long honey-colored hair is catching bits of sunlight, and glinting here and there.

—Whose car is this? we ask.

—We don't know, we boosted it, says Miss Debutante, which is how I think of Boo. Jaime is tall and handsome with dark, heavy eyebrows. He wears blue jeans, an old black T-shirt and a purple beret. His skin is tawny, perfect.

—Are you out of your minds? we laugh.

—It's okay, we're going to take it back in a little while, says Boo. Mostly I am impressed that Boo, who has just finished her freshman year, is hanging out with Jaime, who's in law school. Or maybe he's dropped out, after the shouting, the cops running into Hamilton and Mathematics Hall, New York City's finest, billy clubs swinging. One girl who lived down the hall in my dorm said the pigs taped over their badge numbers so no one could report them for brutality. The day after the bust I saw people I knew from SDS and their fellow travelers walking around campus with bandages or their arms in casts, or their glasses' frames taped together, but I couldn't believe that cops would conceal their badge numbers or that the university administration called the police in to get everyone out of the buildings after all those days of the occupation, which is what we called it.

So now it's a couple weeks later and Paul and I have already been down to Philly and had these screaming arguments with my parents. They didn't understand why students were protesting, and they certainly didn't get the part about the sit-ins in university buildings. Gandhi, we said, Martin Luther King, you see, nonviolent protests against the military industrial complex.

—Bull crap, my dad said. It's trespassing. I saw the picture in *Life* of that kid with the long hair, smoking a cigar, sitting at the university president's desk. Wore sunglasses. We didn't send you to an expensive college, eighteen hundred bucks a year, to be around the likes of those boys. You should've stayed at Mount Saint Agnes. Waste of money sending you up there with all those Commies.

—We're moving in together, we tell my parents. My mother cries, and my father pushes himself up out of his armchair and leaves the room. Paul and I take the bus back to New York and I move what few things I have out of my dorm room and into the sparsely furnished basement apartment. My mother keeps calling me and crying over the phone, telling me I'm ruining my life. Then a couple of weeks later, she starts writing to me saying they won't pay my tuition if I'm going to live in sin. Paul's parents are busy with their own problems, so we don't hear much squawking from them.

So here we are, Paul and I, talking to Boo and Jaime who've boosted a car, temporarily, they claim, and we tell them about our situation.

—Why don't you get married? Boo says.

I tell her I don't think that will work. My parents have been saying since I was twelve that if I got married before I finished college, I'd have to pay for it all myself—tuition, books, room and board—as soon as I slip that wedding ring onto my finger.

Jaime has a better idea. Why not live in the dorm in name only, and live with Paul in the apartment we found?

—That would be a lie, I tell him. And a ridiculous waste of my parents' money. Not everyone's rich like you two.

Jaime laughs, but he gets the point. He knows that he can talk the revolutionary talk all day long but he can always call up his parents for bail money if he gets arrested. Which is exactly what he did the month before, the morning after the bust.

We turn down the ride in the black Caddy and make our way back to the apartment, half of it on street level, half basement, since it's in a building wedged into a part of West 116th that slopes at a thirty-degree angle towards the river.

Paul cashes his paycheck at the bursar's office that afternoon, no charge for staff. He heads to the Daitch Shopwell at 110th and Broadway to buy ingredients for beef stew. I've watched my father make beef stew but have never attempted it. When Paul turns the key to the metal door of Apartment C and the lock clicks and the door falls open, the room is suffused with a rich, savory smell. I don't realize how hungry I am until now.

Paul lifts the top of a battered aluminum pot and inhales deeply. He checks the stew and thickens it with cornstarch, not flour like my father uses. I taste it and think it needs a little salt. There's a loaf of crusty rye bread with a paper sticker on one end that says Diamond Bakery. We sit on the floor because there's no table or counter. We drink from tall glasses of milk, tear off chunks of bread and butter them liberally, and dunk the bread in the stew. We have no television, only a radio, so we listen to the War Summary on WBAI.

After supper, we turn out all the lights but one and climb into the bed we bought a few days before, a queen size box spring, mattress and metal frame. Single bed sheets that I've borrowed from a girlfriend barely cover the mattress, and there's no mattress pad. We have a thin old blanket Paul has brought back to New York from his mother's house. We open the window that faces the airshaft to let in a little breeze.

—We need curtains, I say. I'll make some this week. Just before we drift off, it sounds like he says, *Let's get married.* It's a pleasant thought, and I say we'll talk about it tomorrow.

Fraternity Row

The door flew open. Two boys, dressed up in slacks, Oxford shirts, ties, and tweed jackets, invited us in.

"You're early," they said. "The band hasn't shown up."

I looked around the front room, checking out the dark wood paneling and fireplace. I thought maybe we had the wrong night.

The taller of the two boys spoke first.

"What college you girls from?"

I was just about to say we were still in high school, when Maria blurted out, "We go to college up in Frederick. We came all the way down because we heard that this house throws a great party."

"Yeah, the brothers here are cool," said the shorter boy. He withdrew a pack of cigarettes from his tweed jacket pocket and offered us smokes. Maria took one, and I followed suit. Kate, who never smoked, smiled sweetly and shook her head.

I was afraid one of the guys was going to comment on how young we looked, but they didn't seem to notice.

"We're on the set-up committee," Tall said. "Stick around up here while we organize everything downstairs. The dancing's going to be in the basement. More room to move around there."

He flung his arms around in an awkward dance. Maria and Kate giggled. I kept listening for the sound of Frankie's band slamming the doors of their old jalopies shut, talking loudly to each other, bumping their instruments, amplifiers, and microphones up the frat house stairs. So far, the street outside was very quiet—no band and no Frankie. I was starting to get anxious.

"We'd offer you a drink now," said Short, but the refreshment committee isn't back from the liquor store yet. So all we have right now is water."

There was a loud knock at the door. Tall opened it, and there stood Frankie, dressed in a dark suit, with a white shirt and a bright red tie. Behind him were the rest of the band, all in the same outfit as Frankie.

Frankie must have asked the rest of the guys to pretend they didn't know me, because when they walked in, none of them made eye contact with me. The frat boys showed the band the way to the basement, and the Sympathetics disappeared down the stairs.

More frat brothers and college girls arrived in a wave, and the whole house—even the large kitchen—began to fill up. The beer and hard liquor arrived, and I heard two guys in the kitchen arguing about how to tap the keg. A long hiss signaled the growing crowd that it was time to move into the kitchen for drinks.

The hum of electric guitars and sound checks—*Testing, one, two, three*—floated up from the basement. I recognized the fragments of a couple bass lines: The Drifters, The Righteous Brothers, James Brown. Maria grabbed Kate and me by the hand and steered us towards the kitchen.

"Might as well have a beer," she said. "If we aren't staying long, we've got to get a running start."

We grabbed paper cups of beer and took our drinks downstairs, standing against the stone wall near the impromptu bandstand, an area between two support posts. There wasn't much room for Frankie and the band to move around, but that didn't hamper them. They started with a fast number, and a few couples started to dance. Six or seven months had passed since the last time I'd heard them play, and I was amazed at how much better they'd become. They played two or three songs, and Frankie said a few words of introduction in between. I could tell he had practiced his patter. The band segued into slow dances, the Righteous Brothers, an Etta James tune. Frankie's silken voice, full of sweet emotion and sadness, found a spot just above the guitars and lingered there. After each fast song ended, there was whistling and hooting from the crowd.

A tall boy in a bulky sweater, his tie just peeking out at the top of the crewneck, asked me to dance. His shaggy blond hair gave him a California surfer look. Not my type, I thought, but I said yes anyway.

"Those colored boys sure can play, can't they?" he said.

I felt myself bristle a little.

"I like the singer best," I said. I felt superior to this guy, not only because I would never use the expression *colored*, I might not even say *Negro* any more. It sounded so outdated.

"He sure knows his Smokey Robinson. And his James Brown is out of sight," I said. Surfer guy gave me a strange look, as though he wasn't sure who Smokey Robison or James Brown were.

"Hey," he said, "I'm Bob. Tell me your name?"

I made one up. "Cassandra," I said, "Call me Sandy." I gave him a fake name because I didn't plan on seeing this guy again. I didn't even want to see him after the next minute.

The Sympathetics played a few bars of their signature break tune. Frankie and the band stepped outside for some fresh air.

Surfer Bob slipped his arm around my waist and edged me back over to the wall nearest the stairs. He asked if I wanted another beer.

"No thanks," I said. I extricated myself from his arm. I really wanted to say, *Hey, I'm with the band, Frankie is my friend, I'm going to go outside with them for a few minutes and shoot the breeze with the guys.* But I knew I couldn't say anything like this. It made no sense to be there, except that I loved hearing Frankie singing, in the dark cellar of this old house, even if I had to be among half-drunk strangers.

I looked around for Kate and Maria. I spied Kate leaning against the wall by herself, nursing her beer with tiny, well-spaced sips. Her mother had trained her to do this, and I thought it was pretty smart. People couldn't bug you to accept another drink if you were holding a mostly full glass.

"Where's Maria?"

"Went upstairs with some guy. She said she wanted another beer."

I thought, Maria's already drunk. Kate and I'll have to call one of our dads to come get us, or we'll have to find some kind, sober person to drive us to her house or mine. We didn't have enough money for a cab, and the bus would take forever.

Kate and I went upstairs, but Maria wasn't in the kitchen, nor the dining or living room. We walked outside to the front porch. Even though it was cold and damp outside, people stood around coatless, smoking and drinking from paper cups. Frankie and his pals were standing in a loose circle on the sidewalk near their cars, swigging Cokes. Frankie caught my eye and gave me a brief, comical army-style salute.

I walked down the steps, close to them. "Great sounds," I said. The guys all nodded. They were cool, they didn't let on that they had met me before at their church gigs.

Frankie seemed so happy to see me.

"Catch you soon," he said quietly. The group on the porch, the beer sloshing out of their cups, were so loud that nobody even noticed Frankie had spoken to me.

"Got to find my friends," I said. I gave Frankie a big smile and went back into the Phi Gam house.

"I'm going to take a look around upstairs," I told Kate. "Maria must be up there somewhere. You check the bathroom on this floor, and the other one in the basement."

Kate shook her head. "I'm coming with you."

I preceded her up the wide staircase, hugging the side closest to the handrail because couples were running down from the second floor. When we reached the landing, we heard laughter and the squeaking of bedsprings through partially closed doors along the hall. I thought I heard Maria's voice. I gestured to Kate to stand back several feet as I knocked quietly on the door.

"Maria? You in there?" I slowly opened the door a few inches. Maria was saying something to a boy who was lying on top of her, his pants and underwear pulled down almost to his ankles. His buttocks were covered with dark wiry hair. Maria's eyes were closed and words were coming out of her mouth, but I couldn't understand her. I saw her sweater pulled up almost to her neck and her large white breasts exposed, the pink bra down around her waist. I shut the door quickly. My heart was pounding. I knew Maria was more experienced than me, but I never dreamed she would have sex with someone she didn't even know.

"Let's go," I said to Kate, "let's get the hell out of here."

Kate looked confused.

I started down the stairs. Kate didn't move.

"We're leaving," I told her. My face felt flushed, and my heart was still thumping in my chest.

All the way downstairs Kate kept asking, "How are we going to get home? I can't call my parents, you can't call your father—"

We rummaged through coats that were pressed together on the standing rack. It wasn't hard to find them, since we were the first to arrive a few hours before and our hosts had hung our jackets at one end of the rack. I handed Kate hers. We slipped out the front door. The couples in the front room necking on the lumpy sofas took no notice.

Outside, the air was cold and sharp. When we exhaled, relieved to have made our escape, we could see our breath.

"Too bad it ended like that." Kate said. "The band was really good."

I felt two ways about Maria. I never wanted to speak to her again, and I couldn't be her friend any more. But I hoped she would get home all right, and I worried because she had done something really stupid.

I said a quick prayer that Maria would take care of herself.

We ran to the corner and caught the Number 3 bus that was coming along just as we reached the bus stop. By the time we got to Kate's house, we'd eaten half a roll of peppermint lifesavers to hide the beer smell on our breaths. Kate's mother was watching TV in the living room.

"Mary Alice needs a lift home," Kate told her. "It was a boring party."

When I got home, my father was sitting at the kitchen table having a snack of milk and pretzels. The comics from the evening paper were spread out before him.

"How was the party?" he asked.

"Oh, so-so, I guess," I said.

He poured me a glass of milk. We divided up the funnies and I read every last one of them.

Going Too Fast

Julia and I are walking down a long pink hall in the nursing home at Woodmere. A Catholic seminary in its former life, it has been transformed into a huge complex of buildings south of Baltimore, a small city of apartments for affluent retirees. We're in the vast assisted living building. We pass a few patients sitting in wheelchairs and nodding at the television. We're here to see Aunt Kate. Julia goes over to the nurse's station and asks for the number of Mrs. Hopkins' room. She steers me by the elbow and whispers, "This is it—her room." Kate is not our aunt, not a blood relation. She's my godmother. Her closeness to us was borne out of my mother's friendship with her. They were just neighbors at first, then they were two women who had their first babies late in life. They became as close as sisters.

I haven't seen Aunt Kate for a couple of years. It's obvious that she hasn't had a perm since then. Her hair, still mostly black with a few streaks of white, is blunt cut, held back in a tiny ponytail. She is in bed, the covers up to her chin. They've put little socks on her hands, impromptu mittens.

"Hi, Aunt Kate," says Julia cheerfully. "We came to see you."

"Oh, dear," says Aunt Kate, looking at us from her lying down position. She starts to cry.

"Oh, dear."

"What's the matter, Aunt Kate?" says Julia, very sweetly, as if Aunt Kate were one of her children, who are still quite small.

"I can't remember." says Aunt Kate, then again. "I can't remember." She continues to cry.

"Don't cry, it's okay if you can't remember. We've brought pictures," says Julia. I am always impressed by Julia's preparedness. Out of her large handbag, she pulls out a binder of snapshots. I know she has pulled these from a dozen large albums. She's made a little anthology for Aunt Kate, just for this visit.

"Here's a picture of you and our mom; that's Sara, our mom," says Julia. It's a photo from a cruise in the 'Seventies. They are wearing long gowns. Kate is more than a head shorter than Mom, and she is wearing a pastel flowered dress that seems to have no shape. But tall, silver-haired, dark-eyed Mom is dressed is a pale green satiny thing. You can see her wonderful figure; the satin hugs her breasts just enough but it isn't too sexy, not cheap looking. She's wearing sparkling drop earrings, rhinestone but you wouldn't know. She looks elegant and happy.

"I can't remember," Aunt Kate says again, and tears are running down the sides of her face towards her ears because she is still lying down. Julia and I pull our chairs closer to her so our faces are nearly touching hers.

"It's okay," says Julia. "You two had some good times together. This was one of them. You were on a cruise. Dad was there too. You three took a lot of trips together."

Aunt Kate lifts her head a bit and looks at us. The look in her eyes changes slightly; she has connected to something from the past that she recognizes. "I know she was my good friend," she says pointing to Mom's image.

"She was your friend." Julia echoes. Now Julia and I are both crying. Aunt Kate is crying too.

I signal to Julia and we get up from the stiff chairs and walk away from the bed for a minute.

"I think we're upsetting her," I say.

"Maybe," says Julia. "Maybe we should get ready to leave soon."

"No, just a few more pictures, some of us," I say.

We sit down again. Julia takes out more photographs.

"Here I am when I was a little girl," she says to Aunt Kate. "And here's one of Isabelle."

"I lived with you for a bit when I was little," I say. "After Daddy had the boat accident, when he was in the hospital. I learned to eat fresh peaches at your house, do you remember?"

Of course, she doesn't, and I don't know why I thought I could jar loose a few cells in her crackled brain so that she would reminisce with me. It strikes me that Julia and I are going through this exercise just to make ourselves feel better about Mom's being gone. I start to cry.

"You were very good to me," I tell her.

Aunt Kate studies the picture for a minute, then looks at me. "You are very big now," she says slowly. "And you have such pretty...glasses." I am puzzled—they're just ordinary wire-rimmed frames.

"Eyes," Julia whispers to me. "She means eyes."

"Thank you," I say, and I lean over and kiss Aunt Kate. She has almost no wrinkles. Her skin is smooth and tawny. It's the Indian blood, I realize.

Julia tells Aunt Kate we must be going. We hug and kiss her again. Julia stops to talk to a nurse in the hall while I pretend to read the notices on a little bulletin board in the hall outside Aunt Kate's room. Julia is taking in information like a social worker. She's so good at getting the straight story from just about anyone. I watch her talking—so animated, her hands moving quickly to punctuate her words. Then she tilts her head fast, towards the door, telling me it's time to go.

"I want you to see one more thing," she tells me. "The chapel. It's beautiful." We walk down the stairs and out the front entrance of the building, past the same smiling young receptionist who gave us directions a half-hour earlier. As we walk out into the cold air, I start crying again, this time with huge sobs and a seemingly unstoppable flow of tears.

"I feel so empty, I feel like my whole life is falling away," I say.

"No, it's not leaving, it's all still here, it will always be here," she says, taking my arm and pressing it against her side." Come on, this chapel is lovely, it will make you feel better to see it."

We enter an old stone building; it must be part of the old seminary. A couple of young guys are sitting behind a desk there too, and they point us down the hall to a new-looking door. There is a little vestibule with a plaque saying how some cardinal began building this chapel in the 1920's but ran out of money before it could be completed.

Inside the chapel is all little mirrors and tiles, on the fat pillars, on the altar floor, just thousands of tiles in mosaics. Statues of angels lean out of the wall above the altar. The place looks like the Roaring 'Twenties, all excess and wealth and showiness.

I am still crying. I sit and think about Mom. Yesterday we went to the funeral home to identify her body before she could be cremated. Her body— her corpse, I had to keep telling myself so I wouldn't think it was really her, lay on a plain gurney, a blanket covering her up to her chin. We had to go into the basement of the funeral home; it was carpeted and painted, but it was still a flight down from the ground floor. Then, Julia and I had to give all the statistical information to the young woman at the Cremation Society desk.

The girl is pleasant and businesslike. When we finish with the forms, she says, "You may see your mother now. She looks pretty good. But we had to clean her up a bit because there was a lot of blood, and some scratches on her face."

My heart starts pounding. Her body looks so small, lying on that gurney. She looks okay, but not really asleep. I keep telling myself, this isn't really her.

Julia starts crying, this time. "It isn't really her," I whisper. "It's just her body, Julia." I don't want to touch the skin. I don't want to feel it cold and stiff; she'd been gone for hours. Instead, I touch her hair. It's soft and so white and thick. I want to go back into the Cremation Society woman's office to borrow a pair of scissors, to take a lock of hair.

"Goodbye, Mom," I say almost in a whisper, and Julia and I hold each other for a few minutes. I look down the long narrow low-ceilinged room at coffins, propped open, revealing lush satin linings. I am glad Mommy is going to burn up in a burst of flame, I think. This is the way she had always planned for it to end.

On the way back to Julia's house we stop at a Dunkin Donuts for coffee. We drink it in the car as she drives home on the beltway. We don't have any music, and we don't say much. Maybe we talk about how much it will cost. Maybe we talk about how long I will stay before I fly home. We speak about how glad we are there isn't going to be a funeral, a Mass or anything. Mom's wanderings through various denominations has made it clear what she didn't want; she didn't want the Funeral Package. Not a Mass. Probably nothing Protestant either. We aren't in California so we can't do a New Age thing. We will have to work something out over the next weeks, something she would have liked.

When we get to Julia's house, she wants to take a long bath. She fills the tub with Epsom salts and pins up her hair. She props her head on one of those inflatable plastic pillows that are supposed to look like a scallop shell. From several rooms away, I hear her weeping. I ask her if she's okay and she apologizes for crying so much. I take her a mug of herb tea and leave her alone. Actually, I'd love to be alone myself right now, in the bath and crying. Instead, I check my email on Julia's old computer but there's nothing there for me, nothing from anyone. Especially, there's nothing from Mike. He's silent from his end in LA. If I could talk to him now, what would I say? *Please make me feel better* sounds so pointless, as if he could do anything anyway.

We have the memorial service weeks later, for Mommy on a sunny day in February. Julia's boys are dressed up in these suits she's bought at the Goodwill store; they look so grown up. Alex plays the violin; he's chosen the Chorus from *Judas Maccabeus*, from his Suzuki book. I play "All Blues" on the piano, with the music teacher from Julia's school on trumpet. Julia reads a poem; all I can remember of it now is the refrain, "I had a mother who read to me." Then Mommy's old protégée Sis gets up and tells some funny stories not even Julia and I had ever heard about Mommy when she was at work. Afterwards, a blur of our friends from high school, the few who stayed in Baltimore, come over and kiss us, and there are teachers from Julia's school, some people from the old neighborhood, and Mommy's handsome young lawyer Al, who's been married three times.

"I just loved your mother," he says. He's got dark brown hair and blue eyes and doesn't look old enough to have been married so many times. Julia has her arm around my waist and is being very sweet. There are flowers from my friend Joyce who lives in Washington State, and two of our old nuns, our teachers from high school are there, wearing civvies as Dad called them, regular middle-aged lady outfits with printed flowers, sensible shoes. When we get home, we spend the afternoon sitting and eating with our old neighbor Mrs. Frank, who has driven up from her retirement home in Annapolis. She is a laid back, chatty woman who doesn't seem in a hurry to leave like everyone else. After she finally goes, Julia points to the box with Mommy's ashes on the top of the CD player and says, "In the spring, we have to decide what to do with these."

But that spring, we can't decide. Once, we asked Mom where she wanted her ashes scattered. Dad's we put in the Choptank River, where he used to fish. Julia and I drove to the Eastern Shore one day in August with her boys. They were still small then, and we walked out on a stone jetty Julia had found on the way back from Ocean City. We were near the place where our father had fished many times. We told the boys what we were about to do, tried to explain that the ashes would be more like chunks than the ashes they were used to seeing in the fireplace, and we opened the tin. We each took some and strewed them on the water. The current was swift. It seemed to take a short time to do what we had come so far to do. On the way back, we stopped and bought watermelon and corn.

But Mom always said she hated the water; in fact, she was a poor swimmer and afraid of it.

"Oh, just put me in the garden," she would say. But which garden? What if Julia sold the house and moved? Of course, she would move eventually. Where could we scatter those ashes that would be a timeless, forever spot? And why did we fool ourselves into thinking that even the sea was some timeless way to dispose of their remains? I had no garden to speak of either, and we might not stay there forever anyway. So, the ashes sat on top of the CD player.

"Mom liked music, let's leave her there awhile," Julia said. Really, I was happy she was taking care of them, I would be uncomfortable with them in my house.

It's been three or four years now and I think Julia's moved Mom around a few times. Right now, she's in Julia's bedroom, near the books. Maybe this spring we can finally figure it out. Or maybe we will just wait twenty years.

"It's going so fast," Mike said once as, we spoke about our work and our lives and all the books we'd read and talked about with each other. I remember that he was standing up and I was sitting on the green sofa, at his old apartment on West 104th. It was years ago. He took my face in his hands for a minute, looking down at me. Again, he murmured, "It's going all too fast."

It was early summer, and we went for a walk then, in the golden light.

Tony Bennett, Aldous Huxley, and Eddie

What every Baltimore teenager longed for was an unchaperoned week in Ocean City with friends. Lots of friends. Six to a hotel room meant for two. Coke or coffee and doughnuts for breakfast, and maybe a slice or two of pizza for lunch. Dinner was on the fly, as well—takeout or a Dairy Queen burger. There was beer. Lots of it. And there was sex—or what passed for it. The girls didn't talk about it much, but you knew, or thought you did, what a girl was up to. The guys might've been just as secretive, or else they could've exaggerated how far they'd gone. Most of us had to wait until we had graduated from high school to get permission to go to the beach unchaperoned.

My girlfriends and I lined up summer jobs, and we told our employers we couldn't start until the end of June. We were ready to cut loose after our first year of college. My friend Robie, a tall, slender blonde with a quirky sense of humor and a major smoking habit, drove a little red Ford her parents had bought her when she decided to go to college in town. Five of us squeezed into the car. We blasted the radio and sang along as we motored out of Baltimore down to the Bay Bridge and across to the Eastern Shore. Suddenly, cornfields lined both sides of the highway and then I noticed black teenaged boys walking along the road, shirtless, in overalls and straw hats.

The boys were a year or two ahead of us, all dayhops at the local Jesuit college, and we had planned our Ocean City getaway with them in mind. The leaders of this pack were a couple of brothers, both middling lacrosse players. Richie was fair, dark-haired and nervous. Eddie, a year older, had dark Mediterranean skin and a hint of red in his chestnut hair. Eddie was super smart, a math whiz, and quick-witted. He drank more beer than any of the other guys and never stopped talking. A devotee of Tony Bennett, he knew all the words to the most obscure old songs, verses and chorus. He fancied himself a student of literature as well, and quoted Aldous Huxley, Stephen Spender and Evelyn Waugh. Eddie was fine if he had three or four beers, but when he went past seven or eight he got sloppy. I preferred him sober. The four-day stay was fun—for a while. There was lots of beer, and impromptu dancing on the beach and in motel rooms to music from someone's portable radio. We made last minute bargains so that a girl and a guy could have a little private time— never more than an hour. There were unwritten rules: don't hog the room, don't leave your towel on the bathroom floor, hang up your swimsuit if it's wet, and if the beer runs out, get more, if you had a fake ID. If not, find someone who did, and never forget to refill the cooler with ice.

The girls stayed in two adjacent rooms at the Oceanside, where the management didn't care how many people occupied one room. The place had barely survived a hurricane a few years before, when the roof was ripped off by a fierce wind, so I guess they figured a bunch of twenty-year-olds couldn't do much worse. The renovated motel looked pretty flimsy, but it was clean, and the police kept it reasonably quiet. They routinely swooped down after 1 a.m. to caution us, "Keep the noise down, folks."

Eddie and his friends were ensconced nearby at the French Quarter, which had a better pool, nicer towels and daily maid service. None of us swam in the pool, and few of us ventured into the surf. Not much of a drinker, I sat on a blanket on the beach, carefully covering up my pink and white-checked two-piece bathing suit with a T-shirt after I'd been in the sun for forty minutes. My mother had warned me that the sun would ruin my fair skin, and she had nursed me through bad sunburns when I was younger. By nineteen I'd learned my lesson. I sat and smoked Newports and drank lukewarm diet Coke.

More than once, I waited for Eddie for hours, even though he'd given me the rendezvous time and place the night before. Sometimes he stood me up. Or he came late, always with his group of followers, three or four of them in tow. I couldn't get him to separate from them. I wanted a walk—a long walk along the shore our feet in the water, maybe holding hands as we walked past jetty after jetty and talked about elegant mathematical solutions, Aldous Huxley, and Camus. Saturday morning, the two of us sat down to a full breakfast—he had pancakes and sausage, orange juice and coffee, what Tony Bennett sang about. I had black coffee and toast. What I wanted was not the simple life Tony Bennett sang about, but a great big love affair, and what Eddie wanted was a brief encounter, no strings. I wanted gazing into one another's eyes, staying apart from the rest of my friends and his, drinking red wine out of glass goblets and watching the orange sun set over the bay. He wanted to be with his boys, making sure there were always a couple of cases of Bud on ice.

My notions of romance came from the movies—Natalie Wood and Steven McQueen, Richard Burton and Liz Taylor, Julie Christie and Dirk Bogarde. My notions of sex came from a paperback marriage manual that Suze had bought in a downtown bookstore. It contained such useful information as, "When the man is on top during intercourse, the woman might wrap her legs around his waist and when he reaches orgasm, squeeze his buttocks." Eddie's ideas about women must have come from his friends. They flitted from one girl to the next. If the girl was easy, the guy took what he wanted and moved on. If the girl withheld her favors, the guy moved on. None of them, least of all Eddie, was ready for what I had in mind, grownup love and grownup sex.

On Monday night, I went straight for the bottle of tequila, and drank it straight over ice with salt around the rim of the glass. I soon found myself climbing up from the bench along the edge of the boardwalk to the rail above it and trying to tightrope walk in my inebriated state, then quickly losing my balance and falling. Robie caught and steadied me, walking me back to our motel, where I passed out on one of the twin beds. I awoke the next morning in the bathtub, cuddled up with pillow and blanket. I tossed my makeshift bedding out of the tub and took a hot shower, then slipped into my best Bermuda shorts and a white halter top that I thought showed off what little tan I had.

Tiptoeing past my sleeping friends, two to a bed, I walked next door to the French Quarter and knocked on the door. Eddie's brother answered my knock, and I told him to get lost. The radio was playing softly and it looked as though no one had slept in two of the beds. Eddie was sitting on the third bed, and the sheets were rumpled and twisted. He wore a white towel wrapped around his waist. His skin was golden brown from the sun, and his arms and chest muscled from the construction work he was doing that summer. He had trouble looking me in the eye. I sat next to him, took his hand and leaned against him. He smelled of Ivory soap. He lit a cigarette, not bothering to offer me one. He couldn't be with me, he said, because he'd just spent the night with my friend Suze. Suze! Suze of the golden hair, green eyes and high cheekbones, small-breasted but with the best legs. She had an older boyfriend she'd been sleeping with for two years, and she'd left him back in Baltimore at his well-paid, full time job. How dare she. How dare Eddie.

Eddie and I were supposed to go out to dinner at English's Chicken House that night, a date we'd made on our first day at the beach. "The least I can do is take you to dinner," he said.

"Oh, sort of a consolation prize?" I asked him. "Forget it, Eddie. The Chicken House is off!" I hollered. I stomped out of the room, making sure to slam the door extra hard.

The strong sun warmed my back as I walked away from the motel. The ocean's perpetual rhythm was in the background, calling me in for a swim, but all I thought about was catching the bus home. I wanted to sleep in my own room, in my own bed, without six or seven people tramping in and out all night long. I wanted to eat real food for breakfast instead of making do with cigarettes and coffee.

I saw Eddie a few times after that and I tried to be cool, standoffish.

When my parents went away for the weekend, he came over and spent the night. It was what I'd wanted for so long, but he left before dawn the next day, hitchhiking home. I longed to be with him, but sometimes told him I was busy when I wasn't. A few days before I left for Michigan, we sat on my back steps looking out into the small backyard. I only half heard the cicadas' constant hum in the background. Eddie said he couldn't trust me because I was on a quest for experience.

"Who isn't?" I asked him.

He said he was afraid that if we kept on, I might get pregnant and trap him. I was incensed. Why would he think I wanted to get married when I had college and my whole life ahead of me? Why would he think I would want to be with an alcoholic in training? I knew all about contraceptive foam, and Suze, once we'd made up, showed me exactly how to use it.

Eddie and I wrote to each other that fall, letters full of ordinary details and literary allusions. When I came home for Christmas break, he surprised me by meeting me at the bus station. He wore a coat and tie because he was working holiday hours at a department store to make extra money. He dropped me at my house and then went back to work. A week later, he took me to a dance at his school, and to the ratty downtown apartment he and the guys had rented, the place they went to drink. The furniture was losing its stuffing through slits in the old upholstery, and the bathroom was the dirtiest I'd ever seen.

The last time I saw Eddie was two days after New Year's at Robie's. He brought another girl. She told me she was studying to become an esthetician. I wore my little black cocktail number and felt overdressed, when I had aimed for sophisticated. At first, Eddie ignored me, then for a moment, he met my eyes. I smiled a tight little smile, then turned away. You win, I thought.

I kept on with my quest for experience. What sticks with me most are Eddie's lines from Tony Bennett and Aldous Huxley, and my fear of walking like a tightrope artist on boardwalk railings.

Peaches

We were pretty good Catholic girls, never in trouble for anything more than doing a halfhearted job of washing the dinner dishes or taking out the garbage cans for the Monday morning collection. It was late August, and Suze, Maria and I were about to start our junior year at St. Mary's. I had passed my driver's test in June. Suze had her license, too, but on this particular night, her parents had revoked her driving privileges for two weeks for some minor infraction. Her father had been in the military, and he liked to run his family like it was the army.

School was starting in eleven days. I was determined to make the most of the summer's end. I left my family's station wagon parked in front of Suze's house on Northwood Drive, wedging it between a couple of her neighbors' cars. Suze grabbed her house key and called down to her mother who was ironing in the basement, "Be back later, Ma." We hustled out by way of the kitchen door, past the trash cans at the end of the cement walk, out the gate and down the alley route to Maria's.

Mrs. Selig opened the door. Grey haired, stern, and a little hard of hearing, she never wore makeup. I guess she always made me feel a little on edge. My manners weren't good enough for her. She wore an apron spattered with shards of red and yellow fruit. The odor was sweet and fragrant, almost overpowering. But for a change, Mrs. Selig seemed happy to see us. She even smiled a little as she poked her head into the dining room and said, "I hope you like peaches, girls. Come on in—Maria and I are just getting them ready for freezing."

In the small kitchen, ripe, fragrant red and gold peaches were piled up on the counter and the table. They spilled out of plastic containers, china bowls, and a half-bushel basket. Maria wore shorts and a sleeveless blouse, her dirty blond hair pulled back into a ponytail that she'd pinned under so it looked like some kind of French hairdo. For a few minutes Suze and I just stood there and watched Maria slice peaches for the freezer. A long, flat peach cake still in the sheet pan cooled on a rack on the table next to crockery bowls of peaches. Mrs. Selig peeled fruit after fruit. She removed the skin from each one and wiped her hands on her apron.

"I'll finish up," Maria said to her mother. She flashed and me a look, as if to say, *I wish she would just leave*. "Meg and Suze can help."

Mrs. Selig sounded pleased and annoyed at the same time. She took off her apron and folded it carefully over the back of a chair. She told Maria, "Just be sure you wipe off all those counters, hon, so I don't feel anything sticky when I come in later on to make your father's lunch for tomorrow." She strode off towards the living room and we heard her switch on the TV.

"Did you bring the money?" Maria asked me.

"Right here," I said. I patted the front pocket of my shorts.

"How much?"

"Thirty," I said, reaching into my pocket and pulling out three tens and laying them on the table next to the peach cake. "Enough for all of us and more."

"More is good," said Suze. "We can always sell what we don't want."

"You want to walk down there or what?" Maria asked Suze and me.

"Let's drive," Suze said.

"No way." I was always paranoid about the car. "If anything ever happened to my dad's car—that neighborhood—"

"So what are we gonna do, take the bus?" Suze asked. It was pretty obvious what a stupid that idea was.

"Very funny, Miss Schmitter," I said.

"Let's call Bill Nash and make him drive us," said Maria.

"Right, sure, Mr. College Boy is gonna drive us down to Thirty-Third Street," I said.

"Like in what, his mother's Dodge Dart with the push buttons?"

"Who cares if the car's not cool? He's cute," Maria said. "Let's call him."

"Let's walk," said Suze, "Bill's so boring."

"You just hate him because he never asked you out," I said. "Not that your mom would let you go out with a guy in a car." He'd never asked me out either, but I wasn't going to let that stop me from giving Suze a hard time. She shot me a pissed off kind of look, but she didn't say anything, probably because she knew I was right.

"How about we go get your car, you drive us, you drop Maria and me off at Thirty-Third Street and you wait in the car for us?" Suze said. "No big deal, Meggy. It would take about ten minutes."

I hesitated. It was only seven, and it would stay light for a while yet. Where we were headed wasn't such a great neighborhood, especially after dark, but we had plenty of time to get down there and back. And the last thing in the world I wanted to do was call Bill Nash for a ride anywhere. It wasn't that I didn't like him. I'd had a minor crush on him since the beginning of tenth grade, when I saw him play a small role in a De La Salle play. He was the guy constantly stumbling in drunk and falling down in "You Can't Take It With

You." The play was stupid and I didn't remember a thing except this tall boy with rosy cheeks and a shock of dark brown hair, crashing to the floor and causing waves of laughter from the audience, especially the girls. Since then I'd heard that he and his friends from grade school had won a couple of CYO drama contests, only this time, for serious stuff. Now he was in college, and I wondered if he had a girlfriend. Probably some older girl—no way he'd be interested in a high school junior.

"Are we going or not?" Suze asked. "I need a smoke. Now."

Maria's parents didn't allow smoking in the house—at least not for kids. It was fine for them to smoke, of course.

"Let's get out of here," Suze whined.

"Fine. I'll drive," I said. It would be good to have some fun for a change. The whole summer had been nothing but boring—working at my father's store, mowing the lawn, driving around at night with my girlfriends wishing we had someplace to go—a party, maybe to D.C. where it was legal to drink if you were eighteen, maybe hang out with some older guys. But all we had so far was the movies and if we were lucky, someone with a house on the shore invited us down overnight. Once Wanda Bobenko invited us to a cookout at her family's place on the Severn, but we only put up with her because at school she tried to sit at our lunch table. Eventually, we just caved in and Wanda started thinking she was one of us. Needless to say, she wasn't.

"I'll ask if I can go with you," Maria said. She crossed her fingers and held them up. Suze tapped her foot loudly and sighed as Maria wiped her hands, threw the dish towel on the kitchen table, and walked into the living room.

"Let's wait on the back steps," Suze said. "I bet her mom says no way." She pulled her cigarette pack out of her shorts pocket and tapped one out. "You want one?" Very quietly, she opened the door for me and we sat down on the concrete stoop.

"Sure," I said. I wasn't a regular smoker but sometimes it just felt right to have one. Suze pulled out a silver lighter. She lit my cigarette and then hers. She inhaled and started blowing smoke rings. Fully aware that I'd not yet mastered that skill, I took a long menthol-soaked drag and just blew it out slowly.

"Nice lighter," I said. "Where's it from?"

"Copped it from my sister," Suze said. Her sister, Catherine, was in college. She had a summer job waitressing in Rehoboth and had left most of her good stuff at home in the room they shared. "I have to put it back before she gets home next week."

"Don't lose it or she'll kill you," I said. Catherine was a notorious bitch and very particular about her possessions, especially the expensive gifts she got from boyfriends, of which she had many.

"Fat chance," Suze answered. "I have the goods on her. She and her friends had a party when my parents went away that weekend and I helped her clean up after—so now I can use all her stuff and she can't stop me."

Just then, Maria practically ran out her back door. She grabbed us each by the wrist and pulled us down the narrow concrete walk and through the gate. Letting go of us for a moment, she swung the metal gate hard behind her to close it tight.

"My mother is so damned annoying," she said, looking back over her shoulder. She'd unpinned her hair and it fell past her shoulders. "Get a move on, you two!" she laughed, and she bumped her hip lightly, first against me, then against Suze. "I made parole, but the Queen says I have to be home by ten-thirty."

"You poor kid," I said. "My summer curfew's midnight."

We started singing as we walked three abreast down the alley, loud and bold like Martha and the Vandellas about how this man had nowhere to go to evade our teenage passion. The singing ended abruptly as we dissolved into laughter, about nothing. Sweat ran down my face and dripped into the front of my sleeveless top. My hair, which I had worked so hard to straighten that afternoon, began to frizz up. I pulled it back as tight as I could and secured it with my headband, trying to look as cool as Maria.

We cut through the end of the alley and turned on to Northwood Drive. As we walked, we saw children everywhere—little kids carrying empty screw-top jars with holes poked into the metal tops. They ran across front lawns, squealing and catching lightning bugs. Some girls were lining up at the curb by the ice cream truck. The Good Humor man, a short, dark guy dressed in whites, with his change-maker at his belt, pulled popsicles and rockets from the truck freezer. Wisps of dry ice smoke escaped from the open door in wisps.

"Want a popsicle?" Suze said. "I sure do."

"Not now, we have to get moving," I said. "The guy told me he'd only be there till eight, and he might not stay that late."

The guy was someone called Steve. A girl who lived up my block, Doris, told me about him. I used to ride bikes and play hopscotch with Doris back in grade school, but now she went to the Vo-Tech and ran with a tougher crowd.

At the bus stop on school mornings, she and I would sometimes talk about boys, makeup, and hair styles. She was studying to be a beautician, and she always carried this shiny plastic case with all her supplies, curlers, end papers for perms, special equipment that hairdressers used. For several weeks while we waited for the bus, we talked about where it was easy to buy beer, how to get fake IDs, where to get diet pills and grass. She knew a lot about all this, and I knew practically nothing, but I knew I could get some good leads from her. One day she wrote down Steve's phone number down for me on a scrap of paper torn from the top of a magazine. Advertisement. She gave me some advice. "This is where you want to go if you want grass," she whispered to me one afternoon as we both sat waiting for the bus. "Down near the Waverly Theatre is where he hangs out. He's not a sleaze, he won't rat you out. He's nice. And sort of cute, for an older guy," she had added. Her express bus pulled up just then as she handed me the piece of paper, with Steve's name and number scrawled in her round handwriting, all its i's dotted with circles. She stepped up to the token box, dropped in her fifteen cents, and looked back at me for a split second. She was scaggy-looking, with her teased blond hair, pink lipstick, and too much black eyeliner. But on her, it looked almost cool. She was tall and thin and knew how to carry it off. She knew that everyone else knew it, too.

"Hey, daydreamer, I have dibs on the death seat," Suze was saying. She opened the passenger door of my car and climbed in.

"Fine with me, age before beauty," Maria said as she slid into the back seat. "Thirty-third and Greenmount, driver," she said.

"Are we sure we want to do this?" I asked.

"Are you turning chicken on us?" Suze said.

"No way," I said, as I started the car and pulled out into the street. Suze switched on the radio and started fooling with the dial.

It was quiet when we arrived on the block where Steve had said to meet him. I had called him from a payphone earlier that day.

"Bring cash, thirty bucks minimum," he said when I phoned him. "You have to take my word on it. You don't get to try the stuff first," he told me. "Anyone asks, you don't know me."

"See if you can find number 505," I asked Suze. She rolled down her window and peered out.

"This is the six hundred block. One more block west. You're not getting weirded out, are you?"

I maneuvered the station wagon into a parking place, not a legal one, near a fire hydrant.

"Should we get out and wait for this guy, or stay in the car?" Maria asked.

"Don't be stupid. We stay here. This isn't the best place to be, even in daylight," Suze said.

"Looks fine to me," Maria said.

"You're so damned naïve," I said. "You two stay here. I'll check to see if this guy's around."

Just then the front door of one of the houses flew open, and out walked a guy, a lot older than us but not as old as our parents. I'd say he was maybe thirty. He was dressed in jeans and a T-shirt, really dark blue, with a pack of cigarettes peeking out of the pocket. Winstons, I think, or Marlboros, a red-and-white package.

"You Meg?" he called down to me from the doorway. He had dirty blond hair and blue eyes, and very strange little teeth, pointy at the ends.

"That's me."

"You girls want to come in for a sec?" he asked.

I turned to Suze and Maria. Maria had a weird expression on her face, a look as if to say, *No way*.

"Well," I said. I hesitated.

"Come on up. I need a few minutes to get it together for y'all."

He seemed sincere enough, but I didn't know if we should go in. I mentally ticked off the pluses and minuses: bad neighborhood, a guy we didn't really know, no information about who was in the apartment already. Plus, we were obviously about to engage in a criminal activity—buying illegal drugs.

"No, thanks," I said, smiling weakly. "We'll just wait here."

"Have it your way, babe," he said, and disappeared into the apartment.

"Hey, Meg, maybe we should go and buy some beer," Suze said. She sounded nervous.

"Yeah, right," I said. "At your age, sure. Good luck."

"No, really." Now Suze sounded annoyed. She waved a card she had pulled out of her back pocket. It was a Delaware driver's license. "I have ID."

This was something new. "From where?"

"What does it say?" Maria asked.

Suze read, "'Mary Ellen Steele, 4015 Walnut Avenue, Wilmington, Delaware.' One of my sister's many fakes."

"Suze, we don't need beer," Maria said. "What we came for is better.

Anyway, we don't need them both, that's for sure."

"Stay put, Suze," I said. "Don't move the car. Wait right here." I fixed my eyes on Steve's front door.

"Hey! Get up here, Meg!" Steve had reappeared at the screen door of his place. I could barely make out what he was saying.

"You coming up to do this or not? Who else is coming with you?"

He smiled. I noticed for the first time that he had a dark green tattoo, maybe a gargoyle, on his forearm. His jeans were really tight, with thin lines of grime running horizontally across the thighs, as if he were a mechanic of some kind.

I glanced over at Suze and Maria.

"Who's going up with me?" Neither of them said a thing. Suze jerked her chin up and over towards the porch where Steve stood.

"OK," I called up so Steve could hear me.

In a lower voice, I told Suze and Maria, "Lock all the doors. No. You sit in the driver's seat, Suze. Keep the keys in the ignition."

Suze got out of the car on the curb side, locked the door, and walked around to the driver's side. She slid in behind the wheel. When she leaned over and rolled down the front passenger window, I tossed in the keys.

"I'll be right back," I said.

I ran up the steps to the porch and stopped a couple of feet away from the front door. Steve had just lit a cigarette, and taking a long drag on it, he said quietly, "How much money you girls bring?"

"Thirty," I said.

"Lemme see it," he said in a low voice.

"Where's the stuff?" I asked.

"Don't you worry about that, lemme see the money," he replied. He started to move towards me a bit. From the inside of the house I heard a radio playing music, country music. I hated country music.

"Okay." I started to reach into my pocket.

"Wait a second, Steve—" I said.

"I ain't Steve," the man said quietly. "Come here now and gimme that money."

My heart began to beat faster.

"You're not Steve?" I said. I felt my face flush. "Who are you, then?"

"Just give me the money, darlin'," he said.

My hand stayed jammed in my pocket, and I froze. He reached over and grabbed my elbow with one hand, squeezing it hard, while his other hand seemed to go into his back pocket. My heart started thumping faster, the noise of that heartbeat rising in my throat first, and then in my head.

I jerked my elbow away. Surprisingly, he was so unsteady on his feet that I easily stepped backwards a few steps and started for the stairs, while he stood there seeming dazed.

"Get back over here," he said in a flat voice, as I felt my foot touch the top stair and tried to propel myself down.

"I got what you came for." He started down the stairs after me. I reached the bottom of the stars and nearly tripped across the sidewalk. I pounded on the passenger door window and Suze leaned over and pulled up the door lock.

"Drive!" I screamed, as I got into the car. "Drive! He's coming! Drive, you idiot!"

Suze started the engine and pulled into the street, tires squealing. We rode in silence—no radio, no talking, my heart still pounding. I wound down the window halfway and heard that familiar whooshing sound as we quickly passed parked cars, one after another.

"You okay, Meg?" said Maria quietly from the back seat.

"Yeah, I guess," I said. Then, I said, "No, actually, I'm not."

"What happened, he try something?" Suze asked.

"I don't know what was going on. He didn't have the stuff, I don't think. God, he was so disgusting—"

Maria lit a cigarette, took a drag and handed it to me. "Here, you need this," she said.

"Thanks," I sucked in the mentholated smoke and exhaled slowly. "Maybe Doris Kozak set the whole thing up, that scag."

"You should be more—we should be more careful," Maria said. "If my mother knew I was down here—"

"Let's leave your mother out of this," I said.

"You really think Doris might have set us up?" Suze said. "You're okay, aren't you? That guy was a jerk. How old do you think he was, Meggy?"

"Ancient. Maybe thirty? Thirty-five?"

We began to giggle and then we couldn't stop.

"Turn on the radio," I said, when we finally quieted down. "Let's go back to someone's house and watch TV." Neither of them said a word. We drove on past the stadium and onto the boulevard heading north.

A few blocks away from her house, Suze said, "I'd better pull over and let you take the wheel. My father will ground me for another month if he catches me driving."

"We could drive by Bill Nash's house," Maria said. "His mother works nights."

"What was that creepy guy trying to do, anyway? Suze asked.

"I don't know, take our money, I guess," I said morosely. "Maybe something worse. Forget it, Suze. I don't want to talk about it. Maria's right, let's ride by Bill's."

Suze parked the car as near to Bill's house as she could, considering the cars were wedged bumper to bumper all along his block. We rang the doorbell. Bill appeared, tall and smiling, wearing cut-off jeans and a T-shirt from his old high school.

"Ladies," he said, as though he'd been expecting us. "Come in. Nothing like company on a hot, humid night in the city. *Mi casa es su casa*, as they say. Please join me."

He led us through the house, empty of adults and siblings, and out to the back stoop. We sat there for a couple hours drinking beer, smoking his cigarettes, and listening to the Top Forty hits on the kitchen radio, which sat in the window facing out towards the fenced-in backyard. Suze and Maria sat on the lowest step, tilting back cans of Budweiser into their mouths and looking up at the darkening sky. Clutching their jars of lightning bugs, the last of the children were called in when the streetlights switched on.

Bill and I started to sing along to the radio, and he slipped his arm around my shoulder. The stars came out, and the cicadas began their rising song.

The Real Thing

My father's tavern, a shot and a beer place, sat on the corner of North Kresson and Fairmount Avenue, though Fairmount was not really an avenue, merely a wide cinder stub of a road flanked by Mr. and Mrs. Hall's gritty brown house and the corner building, the one that housed the tavern, the last in a row of Highlandtown houses. This wasn't one of those blocks with the pristine white marble steps you see in the postcards of Baltimore. Kresson Street wasn't that pretty and never had been. The row house steps in that block were wooden, and in various states of disrepair. To walk into the tavern, or the Place, as my father called it, you had to walk up one concrete step, push open a heavy door by half leaning on it, half thumbing down the latch, and go into a long narrow room with twenty-foot high tin ceilings.

When I remember it now, I never imagine it as empty, the way it was early on Sunday mornings when I went to do the bookkeeping. Instead, I envision a half dozen regulars sitting at the long wood bar with its brass foot rail. The men are leaning over their drinks; it's early morning. There's a grayish light coming in through the front windows over the Hotpoint grill, and only a couple of the men are drinking beer or whiskey. The rest are having coffee and breakfast, white oval platters of grilled ham, scrambled eggs, white toast. The black and white TV provides background noise, "The Today Show," with Dave Garroway. The customers ignore the television, on its shelf high above the bar, right over the pay phone.

The scents of cooking ham, stale beer and diesel fuel of Blue Diamond trucks mingle. My father walks to the side door, limping in his leg brace, to take a delivery of beer. One keg is wheeled to the tap behind the bar, at nearly dead center; the others are rolled down to the cellar, by the bulkhead entrance on the side street. I'm never allowed down there. It's almost a certainty that rats live side by side with those cold kegs. Sometimes my father lets Freddy, the mentally retarded guy with the peaked cap who mops up, supervise the unloading. Freddy is full of weird stories about monsters and people who scare him.

"Don't pay any attention to him," Daddy says, "he's not right in the head, you see."

The middle room, next to the bar, has a large poker table with a felt top, always covered up except for Friday and Saturday nights. It will disappear after a few years, after the lease runs out. There's a juke box, with Hank Williams and Jerry Lee Lewis numbers. And there are several square tables, and in the very back, an upright piano, long out of tune. Above it, a black and white sign warns customers: No Dancing. Really, though, no one ever even tries to dance there. The sign is decades old even when I am five, just learning to read the words. In the very back of the building is the kitchen, with deep stainless steel sinks and work spaces, a hamburger press—which will become obsolete in the 1960's when portion control, pre-made hamburger patties from the food industry's laboratories appear—a well-used commercial range, and dozens of large pots and pans hanging on a pegboard that fills the wall. This is where my father makes chili, bean soup, pea soup, and the ham, bone-in, dotted with cloves, patted down with dark brown sugar and dry mustard, and bathed in cheap port wine. Years later, at a bar clear across town in Parkville, ten miles from here, someone will say to my father, "Nobody could make a ham like Charlie Schmidt down in Highlandtown."

And my dad will reply, "Don't you know who you're talking to?"

At the end of Fairmount Avenue, stands a scrap metal yard, and abutting it, the Blue Diamond Truck dispatch station. From the curb where Daddy parks his car at the tavern's side entrance, I can hear the two-way radio static and buzz. Some of the men who work on the Pennsylvania Railroad drive their cars in to Fairmount and angle park them, but most customers just walk here. Forty houses in one block, are bookended by our tavern on one end, and on the other, by Wishnow's bar and packaged goods store. The city bus stops up there on its way to Dundalk. I am never allowed to walk past Wishnow's, and my mother, who prefers that I never go to the tavern with Daddy, doesn't want me to play with Kresson Street children. There is one girl older than me, with a harelip. We play step school with some others, and she appoints herself the teacher. I have a photograph of us on the steps, but I cannot remember any of the other children's names. My little sister is with us, in a white dress with a red collar. It must be spring, because we're not wearing coats.

As I grow older, when I go to work with Daddy, I spend most of my time reading in the big armchair next to the jukebox. More than one customer calls me a bookworm, a word I grow to hate. I sit in an easy chair my father has installed near the juke box in the long second room because he needs to get off his bad leg as much as possible. I read biographies of Presidents and naval heroes, mysteries, adventure stories—a book a day. I have no idea why I am here with him or where my sister or mother are. When Dad and I return home, we have to shower and change our clothes because they smell of smoke and beer.

The regulars were not necessarily regular, nor were they faithful customers; there were about ten of them, but the cast changed weekly. The one I liked best was Mr. Howard Bird. Everyone called him Hats. You may wonder if he wore a hat, and indeed, he did—in the summer, a straw hat, perhaps a fishing hat. He was slim and brown-haired, and he wore glasses that made him look smart. From time to time his wife Miss Hildy tended bar for my father, but she was slow and she probably stole from him as mostly all his bartenders did, skimming cash in the busy times. So often as not, she was a customer, and since women never sat at the bar, she usually brought in a used half gallon pickle jar. My father would fill it with draught beer, make up a price on the spot, and Hildy was off to drink her beer at home. By the time I was in high school, she resembled Rosie the Riveter, her hair poking out at a forty-five-degree angle from her forehead in a helmet-like pouf, and protruding from the back in a dime store hairnet. She always smelled of soap and cheap perfume, and she was always nice to me. I began to feel sorry for her. She grew fatter and fatter with each year, still wearing those tight sweaters, straight skirts and seamed stockings that must have looked so fashionable twenty years before. The Birds had some kids, but I can't remember ever seeing them. In my mind, Hildy and Hats were a childless couple caught in a time warp.

None of this would be particularly important had it not been for what happened one day when I was working with my dad. I was only seventeen, in my last semester of high school. The law said you had to be twenty-one to serve beer or liquor in the city. I was supposed to be washing glasses and fetching things for my father and Whitey, Dad's latest in a never-ending series of bartenders, but as it got busier around noon, I was pressed into service. I'd been watching my father and the others pull drafts for years, and it took me only a minute to master the art of filling a beer glass up to the top without spilling the head and making a mess. I was feeling competent, taking orders, pulling drafts or pouring shots, taking money. The number of customers dwindled towards late afternoon, around four.

The front door flew open and two guys in dark fedoras pulled down low over their faces started yelling. I was holding a ten dollar bill and just about to put it into the cash register. All the time they kept yelling, I wasn't able to distinguish what it was they were saying. I couldn't move.

"Everyone down on the floor," they said. They made Whitey take all the money from the cash register and hand it to the guy who was yelling loudest. They were waving their guns around and screaming, "Nobody move, this is the real thing."

Coke's the real thing, I thought. *What the world wants today Coke is, it's the real thing.* Jesus, it was railroad payday too, which meant extra cash in the register for cashing checks. Now I, too, was down on the floor, face down, my forearms under my chin so I wouldn't get my face dirty. They were calling now for the men's watches and wallets. I started to tremble a little. My legs were shaking nonstop.

"Stand up," they were saying, and I saw the regular customer Daddy nicknamed Rabbi, Mr. Riley, with a scared look in his eyes, and Paddy Sanders, Bernie Zalitis, and my dad shuffling towards the men's room. As I stood up slowly and shakily, the stranger nearer to me waved the gun at me.

"You too," he said. He herded us into the men's room. "Don't anyone leave here for ten minutes. Do you understand, you bald motherfucker?" He pointed the gun at Daddy's head, really close, maybe four inches away. Daddy nodded, said nothing. Inside me there was a throbbing. I kept expecting to hear an earsplitting noise and see brains fly everywhere. To steady myself I tried to notice things. A toilet seat left up. The walls in need of paint. The sweetish smell of the room deodorizer, a twin to the one in the ladies' room. Out of the corner of my eye I saw a tall white metal condom dispenser mounted on the wall. I read the sign on it: "For prevention of disease only. Not for birth control."

I tried to think of the tune from the Coke advertisement. *I'd like to buy the world a Coke and keep it company, it's the real thing, Coke is.* The door to the men's room shut with a thump that was quieter than the pounding of my heart. Paddy was helping my dad up to his feet. We heard the front door open and then swing shut and we waited. We waited for what seemed a half hour. Then we waited longer. Finally, my heart stopped pounding then but I kept on trembling. I couldn't stop. Somebody called the police on the payphone. They were there within minutes, the uniformed cops, but it seemed we had almost nothing for them, nothing specific we could remember. Two guys, not very tall, not heavy, not thin. They wore hats and raincoats, or maybe topcoats.

A couple of detectives showed up a short time later and took statements from each of us. Paddy told them he knew the guns were German lugers.

"Anyone unusual in here lately, maybe casing the place, Charlie?" one detective asked. My dad just shook his head. He was anxious to get me out of there and home, and he was not looking forward to facing my mother and her wrath.

At home the repercussions were worse than he may have feared. My mother was furious. There were many I-told-you-so's heaped on my father. She went up to their bedroom, he followed, and she closed the door. I could hear her voice, not yelling exactly, but very animated and angry. I strained to hear them that day and many days after that, to find out what they were saying. There was the revelation that this was the third or fourth holdup, not the first. There were murmurings late into the night from their bedroom. On my way to the bathroom for my shower I might catch a phrase or two of Mom's—"inside job," " cops on the take," "she could have been really hurt"—but neither of them would talk about it in front of me. A few times the same two detectives came to our house with binders full of mug shots for me to look at. What could I tell them? Every photo looked like it could be one of those guys, yet none of them really matched my memory of them, all shouting with hats pulled down and black guns pointed at us.

After a week or two, the detectives stopped coming. I went back with my unsuitable older boyfriend, the one I had dumped a few weeks before the robbery. Having him back made me feel safer, and he was willing to listen to me tell the story of what happened over and over. Eventually I told it to him so many times even I became sick of it. Spring came, and the senior prom and graduation, and then a job at Fort Holabird, where I translated petty crimes committed by GIs into code and got paid well for it. The robbery faded more and more into my past. I only spoke about it once or twice, years later, to explain why I should be excused from jury duty. My romance with the boyfriend faded, then slipped away altogether. I started dating a young soldier who was waiting to get his orders for Vietnam any day.

That afternoon of the robbery was the last time I ever set foot in the tavern on a business day. My parents banned me from the premises, with one exception: until I left for college, I was allowed to go down on Sunday mornings to do the books. Early Sundays were quiet on Kresson Street, people sleeping it off, or some of the men working overtime shifts at Crown Cork and Seal. All the bars were closed, though they could have opened up at 6 a.m. if they'd wanted to, the city law allowed that. I only had to check the register tapes, run the expenses, record the receipts, and use the adding machine to do the rest. Most Sundays, as I now remember it, the sun found its way in through the glass bricks and spilled onto the grill and the shiny bar top. The din of talking, the curls of blue cigarette smoke and the clink of glasses were gone. I sat in Daddy's old chair, the one where I used to curl up to read when I was younger. Coffee mug in hand, I tuned the radio to my favorite station, raised the volume, and went to work with a sharp Number 2 pencil, scrupulously inscribing the numbers into the ledger book.

Party in the Soul Kitchen

We had been married a little over a year. Al was twenty-six, four years old than me. I'd graduated from college and was working on my master's in education, about to begin student teaching in Washington Heights. Al had dropped out of school and now worked making deliveries at the university. I convinced him to take advantage of the free tuition at the evening college, and he had recently aced his freshman composition course—with a lot of effort on his part and coaching from me. What he learned most in English 101 was not how to write a strong thesis paragraph, what constituted a run-on sentence, or how to marshal evidence to support his claims. Instead, in exquisite detail, he learned about the Doors, and—as much as one really could learn—about Jim Morrison. Back then, this qualified as a legitimate topic for an English comp paper. Even the professors had suddenly turned hip.

I had always loved The Doors, from the year I met Al at my summer waitressing job. He was the bartender and assistant manager, and I was one of a fleet of college girls interested in making big money. I razzed Al about his conservative politics when I learned he voted for George Wallace in the primary election. I mocked him for his materialistic values.

"How can you stand to be tied down by all those objects?" I asked, parroting a remark I had overheard in the dining hall earlier that year. The teasing soon became flirtation, and by summer's end we were spending every evening after work rolling around on the shag carpet at his sister's apartment while she was away in Reno getting a quickie divorce. Bending to my passionate undergraduate rhetoric, Al sold his sleek black XKE, quit his job, and took his first trip abroad. He planned to attend Jaguar School in England and learn his way around those temperamental British machines. We continued our romance over the next four months with twice weekly aerogrammes and a few emotional trunk calls.

When his sojourn in England ended, Al moved to New York blocks from my college, finding a run-down apartment with two undergraduates on a dicey stretch of West 95th Street. The smell of garlic and fried plantains lingered in the dilapidated lobby of the building. For weeks on end, a handwritten notice on a ragged piece of notebook paper was taped to the wall of the shaky elevator: "Do not leave garbage in elevator. He look too bad.—Super Jones."

Though Al was as straight a guy as one could ever meet, something about Morrison resonated with Al, drew him like a siren. Morrison's alter ego, the Lizard King, his posing and his poetic lyrics, and his defiant, rebellious, in-our-parents'-faces attitude struck a chord with Al. We marinated ourselves in cynicism about the government, the war machine, and our parents' traditional values. Spending several hours on a Friday night sitting around dissecting Morrison's lyrics was nothing unusual in our circle. We thought Jim Morrison was a brilliant poet, not your average rock-and-roller.

When the Doors came to town for several nights at Madison Square Garden, Al bought as many tickets as our modest cash reserves could cover, and went to nearly every performance. I only saw two, because I had schoolwork to do. The Felt Forum was far larger than our usual music haunts—cramped midtown clubs or grubby East Village hangouts. Our seats at the Garden were so far from the stage that the sight lines were poor and the sound distorted. Still, I had to admit, Jim Morrison, in his white flowing shirt and ultra-tight pants, had an uncanny ability to command the attention of everyone in the house. Joints were passed, dope was consumed, men and women alike were enthralled.

Al had met a music editor when he was writing his research paper. She liked him, I could tell, and it made me nervous. She liked him so much that she invited him to an after-hours party the record company was throwing for the Doors at a midtown hotel.

"Of course, you're invited, too," Al said, though I was uneasy about the whole idea. The January night was frigid. Al wore a pastel striped shirt and jeans. Opening the closet, I knew I had nothing good enough for this party. Would it be the red Indian print mini-dress with the enormous bell sleeves, or the lavender double knit with the low-cut V neck? I chose the shortest dress I owned. I straightened my long hair it so that all traces of wave or curl vanished. I glanced over my shoulder at the mirror inside our broom closet. I wished my legs were longer. I slipped into my good coat, and as we walked to the subway, I asked Al to slow down so I could maneuver up the hill, teetering in my high heels.

Strategically planning our arrival for after eleven, we went to the Statler Hilton, then soon learned the party was at the newer New York Hilton. To save subway fare, we walked from 33rd Street to 54th—not so easy in those heels, all the while trying to keep pace with a long-legged husband.

The elevator opened directly into the penthouse. My shoes made a loud clicking sound on the marble floor, as we made our way towards the crowd in a room down the hall. We heard music. Men in electric blue dress shirts and wide ties stood around drinking, talking in animated tones. Al spotted the Doors keyboardist and gave me a nudge.

"Look, there's Ray," he said, as though they'd grown up together. There were young women, lots of them, some in flowing hippie dresses, some in more conservative outfits. We wandered into the adjoining room, where several guests passed a joint around. A man curled up in a fetal position underneath the glass coffee table in their midst.

"What's wrong with him?" Al asked the music editor, who had appeared suddenly, greeting Al with kisses on both cheeks, like the French do.

"Oh, him. He's been smoking opium all night," she said.

I stood in the foyer near the elevator. Al was exploring the penthouse, looking for Jim Morrison.

"I'm not leaving till I meet him," he said. I looked at my watch. Midnight. I was ready to go home. I saw no reason to hang around waiting for a superstar who probably wasn't even in the building.

A long-haired young man in a gauzy white shirt walked towards me, smiling as if he knew me from somewhere else. He extended his hand and gazed right into my eyes I found myself embarrassed, and I looked down.

"Hello," he said, "I'm Jim." I couldn't believe my eyes.

"I'm Joanna," I said, briefly taking his hand but not like a proper handshake. "Nice party. Who're the guys in the shirts and ties?"

Jim Morrison emitted a soft laugh. There was a hint of sleep in his eyes and in his voice. My heart raced. I wasn't sure whether to flee or stay put.

"We're going to see a movie now," he said. "You like Hitchcock? We're gonna watch *The 39 Steps*."

I did like Hitchcock, and had ever since my mother had taken me to see *The Man Who Knew Too Much* when I was nine. In a grad school film course we screened earlier Hitchcock films, *Rope* and *Vertigo*. But I didn't say any of this to Jim Morrison because I couldn't get a coherent sentence out of my mouth.

"Oh, cool," was all I could manage.

At that moment, Al reappeared. Our recollections diverge. He says that he met Jim Morrison briefly, just as I had, but in another room, and that two women whisked Jim Morrison upstairs, complaining that there were no drugs left. I remember that Al appeared in the foyer as I was talking to Jim Morrison, and that I was the one who introduced them. To this day, Al claims he has no memory of any movie, but I distinctly recall the mechanical whirr of the old projector, the damaged black and white print, the rolling of the opening credits, and the first few minutes of the film.

We took in the scene around us. People came and went from the room. The cloying smell of pot was everywhere. We weren't much for smoking dope with strangers. Morrison, the Lizard King, was by now closeted with his girlfriends. We had missed our chance to engage in profound, poetic dialog with him—assuming he was even capable of a lucid thought at this time of night and in his state of stonedness.

"It's time to go home," I said. This time, we splurged on a taxi.

One Night Stand, With Mittens

It was January, and I was back at college after my Christmas break. My boyfriend—a holdover from freshman year when I lived at home and went to community college two bus rides away—had broken up with me in a most vexing manner. I had transferred to an all-women's school a three-hour train ride from home, and in my absence, my boyfriend's heart evidently did not grow fonder. On the contrary, he proved unable to endure the distance, preferring convenience to my physical and intellectual charms. On our last real date together, we danced with abandon to the Temptations, who prophetically sang, "I'm losing you." Alongside us in the gym were his friends and their steady girlfriends, all girls I'd met during my year as a commuter student.

And until two odd things happened, I had no idea that I was losing him. He presented me with a very long black plastic cigarette holder for Christmas. I had ordered the *Selected Poems of Stephen Spender* for him from a literary bookshop. I chose the perfect wrapping paper and blank gift card, and inscribed it with a quotation from his favorite Spender poem.

When we exchanged gifts, I sat on the brocade sofa in my parents' living room holding the flat rectangular box and thinking it might be a necklace or a silk scarf. When I lifted the lid and saw the cigarette holder, I felt the impulse to throw it at him, but I pretended to take it all in good humor.

That was my first mistake, most likely inviting my soon-to-be-erstwhile boyfriend's next move. I threw a party between Christmas and New Year's, inviting his crowd and their girlfriends, plus a few classmates from my high school days. He showed up with a very young woman in tow. Her name was Melissa. She was learning to be a cosmetologist. She was sweet and innocent, and she acted like my boyfriend was her boyfriend. It was a cliché. I clenched my teeth, dissembling, while the party dragged on. Within two days, the cigarette holder was tossed in the garbage can in my girlfriend's back yard, mingled with bunched up wrapping paper, ribbon and other Christmas detritus. I snapped my boyfriend's pathetic little gift in two after I drank four glasses of cheap champagne in Anna's kitchen.

But not before I demonstrated various uses for a plastic cigarette holder: chopstick; hair fastener chopstick; bookmark; cane for a troll; conductor's baton. Then, I broke it two and started crying. Anna lit a cigarette for herself and then one for me. She told me my boyfriend was a jerk, that he was not my type, and that the hair stylist-to-be was a stupid little moron. I tossed back another glass of cheap champagne and told her she was the best friend a girl could have.

I took the train back to New York, feeling rejected, rejectable, and ten pounds overweight. I had finals in two weeks, and I hadn't opened one book since I got off the train a week before Christmas. The paperbacks for my American literature and epistemology classes were untouched. I vowed to subsist on coffee, hardboiled eggs and fruit, to drop that extra avoirdupois, and to snag all A's and A minuses. Men were the very last thing on my mind.

The next afternoon, my neighbor from across the hall rapped sharply on my door. I had been studying for hours, rereading *The Scarlet Letter*, writing up notecards to test my memory of novels, short stories, and the professor's lectures. I couldn't stop thinking back to that last rendezvous I'd had with the Bastard, as I now referred to him. My hair needed a good trim and a shampoo. I was wearing my favorite study outfit, an old gray sweatshirt worthy of the Colgate toothpaste villain Mr. Tooth Decay, and baggy jeans.

"You free tonight?" Rachelle asked brightly. I couldn't imagine what she wanted from me. She was a poli sci major who never seemed to study and earned A's in all her courses. "Time to get out the golden shovel," was her favorite expression, and she repeated it like a mantra in the days before midterms and final exams. She was a petite, curvy girl with a perfect hairdo, large brown eyes, and pale freckled skin. She swore like a sailor, and her room was the most disorganized mess I'd ever seen. Yet she emerged daily from it, with shiny swinging hair, in a perfect wool sheath dress, nylons and heels. She was engaged to Sumner. No one had ever met him as far as I could tell, but when she wasn't preparing to dazzle her professors on tests or papers, Rachelle was packing her suitcase for Boston. She flew there every two or three weeks on a cheap student fare. Sumner was in medical school. The relationship sounded very adult and serious.

"I've got work," I told her.

"Oh, come on, I met this cute guy at a party last week, he's in town just for tonight, and he has a friend," she said.

"What about Sumner?" I asked her.

"It's fine, it's no big deal, just beers and cheeseburgers at the Gold Rail," she said. This bar, on the far side of Broadway, was unfamiliar territory for me. I hewed to the West End, where the politicos and poets drank beer and ate comfort food kept warm for hours on the steam tables. Ginsberg and Kerouac had once claimed the West End as their territory. The Gold Rail was the bar of frat boys and jocks, not my type at all.

I shook my head. "I have so much reading. My hair's really dirty. I'm really not in the mood, but thanks," I told her. I didn't want to admit to her that I had recently been dumped for a hairdresser-to-be.

She wouldn't take no for an answer. "Just a couple hours," she promised. "I met the friend today, he's very nice. Graduate student in English, at Berkeley. From Maine."

I was intrigued. "In English? At Berkeley?" I thought it over for about fifteen seconds.

A few hours later, showered, shampooed, wearing the preppiest outfit I could come up with—pleated plaid skirt, pullover sorority sweater, tassel loafers and tights—I met Rachelle in the hall and we went down the stairs to the dorm lobby where our dates awaited us. Hers was boisterous and big, a football player type. Mine was slender, handsome and bookish looking. I was intimidated, because Jake was 23. I had never been on a date with anyone that old.

The evening was full of beer, pitchers and pitchers of it. I made several trips to the bathroom. I waved to girls I recognized, and they seemed surprised to see me at the athletes' favorite watering hole. Jake told me that he was from Yarmouth, Maine, his mother played the cello in the Yarmouth Symphony, and he hated Berkeley and missed the East. As the evening wore on, Rachelle and her date increasingly ignored us and became more and more absorbed in one another. I became drunker and drunker and found myself laughing at almost everything Jake had to say.

It was a cold night, and at midnight when we left the Gold Rail, I realized I had lost my gloves. Jake wore a toggle car coat, a wool cap, and mittens. "Here," he said, "wear this on your right hand." He handed me one of his mittens. "Now, put your other hand in your pocket," he told me. He did the reverse, and we walked up Broadway, weaving back and forth, my left hand and his right in our respective pockets, while we held mittened hands. He sang some Simon and Garfunkel, and I joined in.

In those days of *in loco parentis*, we had a one a.m. weekend curfew. Couples gathered in the lounge area near the front desk making out more and more ferociously as the time of curfew drew nearer. I had often come in from a movie or the ballet with friends, glanced to the left and been taken aback by the amount of necking, petting and dry humping on those settees and armchairs. I thought it was a distasteful display of undisciplined sexuality, and couldn't understand why these people weren't at a frat house or in someone's apartment, where they could satisfy their every urge out of the public view.

All the way back to my dorm, Jake was asking me to spend the night with him at his friend's apartment. He pleaded.

"No," I told him. "No, I couldn't possibly." I was thinking about how he was going to take a late morning flight back to the west coast the next day. I'd probably never see him again, never hear from him again. I was drunk enough to say that to him.

"What does that matter?" he asked.

We entered the dormitory, and I steered him to the left. The lounge was almost empty, since only a few students had returned from Christmas break. We found a dark corner, far from the lights of the reception area. And there commenced the longest makeout session not leading up to having sex I've ever experienced, before or afterwards. Over and over, Jake asked me to come with him to his friend's apartment. Over and over I contemplated it, presented rational arguments as to why I would not, then second-guessed myself. At one o'clock, the guard at the front desk announced that it was time for guests to leave so he could lock the doors. For a second. I panicked, wondering if I should go back out into the cold night with Jake, or go up to my room.

I said goodnight. He did not seem wholly disappointed that I had refused him. He gave me one more long, sensuous kiss and left.

For a time, I thought about him, his stories of growing up in Maine, his musical mother, his tales of graduate seminars at Berkeley. I wished he had asked for my number, or my last name, or my address. For the next few weeks I checked my mailbox daily, hoping for a postcard from him with a witty comment about Hawthorne or Leslie Fiedler.

Exams came and went, and the new semester began. I began to hang out with three seniors who taught me to drink scotch and play Botticelli and "Who would you kick out of bed first?" We went to the Joffrey Ballet and afterwards to dinner at Larré's on West 56th. We ate escargots and shrimp scampi and drank three bottles of vin blanc. In the spring, we visited the Cloisters museum and they talked about their plans for after graduation. I grew my hair long for the first time in my life, and for my twentieth birthday, my new friends gave me a box of hair ribbons. We shared inside jokes and met for dinner in the main dining hall most weeknights. They stayed on to graduate, and I went home to my next to last college summer, unattached and satisfied with my life.

Crabtown Girl

I was an earnest little girl living near the city-county line. For a long time, my world consisted of family, those people who loved me and looked out for me. I came up in a small circle within Baltimore, back then a vibrant, bustling city with blocks of row houses, well designed city parks with golf courses and swimming pools, and buses and trolleys that could take you anywhere from Dundalk to Windsor Hills to Carney for a quarter and two transfers. I knew early on that I had a lovely smile but was no beauty, and I must have figured out that what I had going for me most was a quickness of mind. Soon, school and the library became my second homes, and I stuck pretty close to them.

Smart girl, my father called me. Smart girl in Crabtown, Baltimore, the Monument City. The trick for me was figuring out how to shuttle back and forth between the world I grew up in and the one I wanted to be part of, a different kind of life, one of books and ideas and contemplation. I loved what I knew best and where I had come from, but I already had one foot on the train, the other stuck on the platform.

The cinder-paved way we lived on in those days was narrow. Everyone had a driveway so it was rare to see cars parked on the street. My family lived at the bottom of the hill, where the neighborhood abruptly changed from residential to mixed use. A brick office building and an alley stood at the corner of the tired little street and the wide road that ran up to the county. Most of the houses on our street had been built during the 'Twenties. Ours was the newest, put up in the midst of the Great Depression. My grandmother had been widowed in her late fifties, and it wasn't two weeks before Bethlehem Steel booted her out of the company house on D street in Old Sparrows Point. She took the life insurance money and some savings and found a contractor, chose a standard Dutch colonial plan, and ordered up a two-family house, with the lower half for her and the upper half for a renter.

By the time I came along, my parents had moved from the Point into the upstairs apartment. I was a solitary child much of the time, watched over by one adult or another, but feeling quite alone. I built houses of twigs stuck into the moss under the stunted old crabapple tree in our yard, where poison ivy spread along the fence and climbed up the back of the abutter's brick garage. I climbed into the makeshift swing hanging from the big maple tree or crawled into the tight space under the porch that opened out from my grandmother's kitchen. I rode my tricycle up the street, but never too far, back and forth from our house to the spot where every Saturday, a teenaged boy who worked as an usher at the local movie house washed and waxed his car until I could see my reflection in the black paint.

The sounds of the street were predictable, a mix of early morning birdsong and the bell of the Number 19 streetcar as it rolled down Harford Road into the city, or up over the county line and around the Parkville Loop, then back for another journey downtown. In summer after supper, I could hear evening sounds through the open windows, china and knives and forks being stacked and washed by hand. As sunset approached, I was called in for my bath. Mother helped me into my summer pajamas and read me a story or two, then kissed me and pulled the sheet up to my middle. A fan whirred from atop my dresser, turning this way and that and keeping the room comfortable. Once my mother left my room, closing the door almost all the way but leaving a sliver of light to reassure me, I would crawl to the end of my bed and kneel up to look out the window into the night. If I were lucky, I'd glimpse a trolley on Harford Road as it moved between buildings and then quickly disappeared. I might see lightning bugs, perhaps the same ones that had evaded me only an hour before when I was outside chasing those tiny golden lights. On these nights, my father sat on the wooden steps that led down from my grandmother's kitchen. He leaned back, saying little, laughing each time I made another catch and opened my hand to deposit the flashing light into the jar. Once, he held one of the bugs in his big hand and pried its little light off with his thumbnail, then stuck the dismembered gold bulb onto my ring finger. I shrieked with delight.

Winter kept me inside in the upstairs apartment, but I had books to keep me company. My mother read to me every night, and slowly I began to put the stories with the pictures and the words. In our living room, we had a small television built into a handsome wood cabinet. Each day I pulled up my little yellow rocking chair and waited while my mother opened the cabinet doors and turned a knob. Slowly, the screen came to life with fuzzy horizontal lines and talking. Then, a recognizable image came into focus, a large man in a cowboy suit, a white-faced clown wearing a tiger striped suit and honking a horn, a freckled boy puppet, and a gallery of children who screamed, laughed and clapped in delight when the man called them the boys and girls in the peanut gallery.

If there were ever visitors, they were mostly family—Aunt Sally who lived downstairs with Grandmother and went to work each day in a white uniform, or one of my uncles, or my godparents who lived across the street in a gray house with a wide porch and a driveway, two tracks of beaten down grass under a tree. Once a week a lady came to our house to clean the apartment and do the wash. She wore a blue dress and a white apron. She smelled like the same soap I had in my bath each night, a white cake with letters etched on it. The soap floated and left a faint milky trail after it sat in the water for a long time. When my fingers were wrinkled, Daddy said it was time to get out. I cried when I had my hair washed, and again when my mother combed it out. Rats, she called the tangles. She said I had rats in my hair.

On Sundays my father disappeared for a time, but he wasn't at work. Gone to church, my mother said, when I followed her around the house asking his whereabouts. He'll be back in a while and he'll bring Vienna bread and tarts from the bakery. He returned with two white bags, a one with crusty bread inside, and one with two tarts, one for me and one for my mother. The tarts were flaky crust wrapped around sweet raspberry jelly, and they were dusted with powdered sugar that coated my hands. My mother cut my tart in half with a sharp knife and put it on a paper napkin. I sat at the kitchen table and ate both halves, sticking my tongue inside each half to lick out the sweet red stuff. My mother wet a dishcloth and wiped my face and hands until the sticky was gone.

We had a gray car with metal lines on the outside, and a shiny bumper in front and back. Inside the car had three pedals, and the front seats bent forward so I could climb into the back. I stood up when my father first started the car and backed out of the driveway into our street, but as soon as he stopped at the corner, where our street met the big road, he told me to sit down because that was safer. I wasn't allowed to crank the handle that opened the window, because that might be dangerous. I sat my dolly on my lap and if she wanted to look out, I held her up to the window.

Sometimes we drove with a destination in mind. In summer it might be the ice cream stand, either the one with the red roof, or the one with a green roof, just across the road. One was called Knox's and the other was called Murray's. We had ice cream in white pleated cups. Instead of spoons, we ate it with little wooden paddles. Sometimes we had ice cream sundaes, and if it was dinnertime we had hamburgers, a bag of them wrapped in waxed paper. We ate in the car, listening to the ball game on the radio. Root for the Dodgers, Daddy told me, because we don't like the Yankees and this is an important game. He taught me to say, "I'm for the Dodgers."

My father walked to work across the big road to Mike Schindler's Café, an old roadhouse with a field stone foundation and a large living space on the second floor. Old Mike had died years before, and his family leased the business to my father and his partner, Dickie Ritz. When my father stopped there on his day off to scoop up the money and take it to the bank, he let me sit up on a bar stool and choose two things to eat. I preferred a small bag of potato chips and a pack of Juicy Fruit gum. As I worked two or three sticks into my mouth, the gum came apart, then gradually disappeared and I swallowed it along with the chips, savoring the perfect blend of sweet and salty.

My father forgot I was there. He stood behind the bar and poured a little glass of brown liquid for a customer, then one for himself, then he and the man both drank it down fast.

What's that stuff, I asked, and Daddy said, That's medicine—'cause when I was little, I got a snake bite. Then everyone laughed, and I couldn't figure out why.

My father liked to lie on the sofa on Saturday afternoons, with his feet in dark socks hanging over one arm of the furniture. He made a pillow with one hand behind his head, and there was always a can of beer within reach of his other hand. He set it down on the carpet near the little skirt along the bottom of the sofa. The sofa was black and white, but my mother called it plaid. Daddy tipped the beer can back and got the last drop out, and then he read the paper, opening it like a tent above his head and then folding it in half. He liked to sleep then, and his snoring, soft and regular, filled the living room. He wasn't fun to be with when he read the paper or listened to the ball game on the radio, or when he slept.

My mother sang as she washed the dishes. If she forgot the words, she hummed, or she sang dah dah dah dah dah. Those weren't real words. She folded the laundry that she brought up from the cellar in a big basket. She ran my bath water in the big tub, and let me use my father's soap, the orange bar. She dried me off with a big white towel and dusted power over me. She carried me into my room and let me choose which pajamas I wanted to wear. Then she opened a book and began to read to me, and her voice, so even and clear, began to make me feel sleepy. It was time to say my prayers, and go to sleep. She sang to me, and tucked me in. 'Night 'night, Sleep tight. Don't let the bed bugs bite.

—What are bedbugs?

—We don't have any. They're just pretend. You won't get bitten, she said.

The days rolled out one after the other. When it turned warm again, I had a birthday. My mother made a cake and there were four candles on it, and an extra one for luck. My cousins Diana and Anne came, wearing pink dresses and shiny black shoes. Aunt Carmel carried a large box with an enormous bow.

Scott from across the street was there with his mother, and the mothers and the kids all wore shiny paper hats. My mother helped me open the presents, a brown teddy bear, a jump rope with red wooden handles, and a doll that closed her eyes when you put her down for her nap and cried when you gave her a bottle of water and then squeezed her belly. Diana and Katherine wanted to hold her and I didn't want to let them, but my mother made me give them a turn. Scott's present was a Ferris wheel that you could wind up and it turned, just like the real kind that we were too little to ride on. Then everyone sang happy birthday to you, happy birthday Mary Alice, and we all had cake and ice cream blocks with three stripes, chocolate, vanilla, and strawberry. We blew on the curled paper favors that unfurled and tooted like a horn. I looked around for the fathers and for my father in particular, but they were nowhere to be found.

I don't know when I first noticed that something was different. It might have been when my mother started taking naps when I did. She would sometimes let me sleep next to her in the big bed in the room where she and Daddy slept. She would fall asleep first, on top of the white bedspread, and I would lie close to her, listening to her breathe and trying to stay awake. I never could, though, and it seemed as though only a few minutes had passed before she was standing over me, smoothing my hair back from my forehead and telling me, wake up, sleepyhead, naptime is over.

I should have figured it out long before I did, that something was afoot, some remarkable change about to happen. One day my other grandmother appeared. She was a stocky, short woman with dainty feet and hands that had bumps on them from rheumatism, she called it. She wore powder and rouge, and she smelled like soap and flowers. Her name was Liza Shockney and she lived up in the mountains near Cumberland. I called her Mimo.

She arrived with a brown suitcase and a smaller box full of bottles and jars of cream for her face. She brought me a yellow dress, and had me try it on.

—A bit too big, she said, but you'll grow into it. She asked me to sing for her, and she told me, I had such a lovely voice.

—It's the Welsh in you. Your great grandmother was from Wales. When you get older I'll pay for you to have singing lessons. You should have a trained voice.

—What's Whales? I asked. I thought of big fish, as in the Bible story Mother had read to me, about Jonah in the belly of the Whales.

—Wales is a country, she said. And the people there are poets, and they all have lovely singing voices.

—Where's Mommy? I asked her.

—At the hospital, but she'll be home soon. Eat your supper.

—Is she sick?

—No, she's fine and she'll be home tomorrow. And she has a surprise for you.

—What is it? A surprise? Tell me, I said

—You'll just have to wait now, won't you? Mimo said.

She didn't read to me and she didn't sing either, but she told me a story of when she was young. He mother had died and her father had married again. The woman was a mean stepmother, just like in fairy tales, and she made Mimo wear a purple blouse and a red skirt to school. All the children made fun of her because her clothes were hideous.

—What's hideous? I asked

—Bad. Ugly.

—I rubbed my eyes and closed them. Mimo tucked me in and kissed me on the forehead, then tiptoed out of the room. I kept my eyes open and saw what looked like strings of beads and diamond shaped things on long strands, in different colors, in the dark. My eyes got heavy, and I drifted off to sleep, wondering when I would see my mother and what surprise she could possibly have for me.

I tried to remember the last time I saw my mother, but I couldn't. I think it was early morning, as I hadn't had breakfast yet. I watched as she packed a small overnight case; she called it a carpetbag. I saw her stuff clean underwear, a hairbrush, a nightgown, and a toothbrush into the bag. She hugged me and kissed me three times, once on each cheek and once on my head and told me to be good for Mimo. She didn't say where she was going, but told me not to worry, that she'd be back soon. When she slipped into her long green winter coat, she had trouble fastening the two big buttons over her middle that had grown so fat. My father waited outside in the car. Mimo was hanging up her dresses in my closet and laying her nightgown out on the other bed in my room.

—Watch those steps, Mimo called to my mother. —Hold that banister, Jeannie.

I ran to the living room window with my forehead against the glass. I watched my mother walk to the curb where my father waited in our Plymouth. As the car pulled away, she looked out the window and blew me a kiss.

Mimo wasn't much of a cook. Daddy and she didn't talk much. Suppertime was very quiet, not like when Mother was there, telling us a funny story about her trip to the Food Fair, or asking Daddy about his day at work. Aunt Sally stopped in one morning, bringing the Sunday comics and sitting down to read them to me. Daddy went to work and then to visit Mother at the hospital.

Then after what seemed like a thousand years, the surprise came home. But not Mother. The baby was tiny, bigger than my Tiny Tears doll but much noisier. She cried when it was time for me to go to sleep at night, and she cried in the morning. Mimo gave her a bottle of special milk, and the baby was quiet then, sucking hard on the bottle and drinking down all the milk, but soon afterwards, she started bawling again.

—You've got to get a baby nurse for this child, Mimo told Daddy.

—Not yet, he said. Let's wait and see. Let's see how Jeannie does.

When I asked where my mother was and why couldn't I go see her, my father told me no children under twelve years of age were allowed at the hospital.

—Your mother is not well, he said. We're praying for her to get better. We knelt down and he taught me to say the Hail Mary, full of grace. I did the sign of the cross, just as he had shown me. At night after Mimo put me to bed and tucked me in, I heard the radio from my father's room, the priest saying the rosary. I knew my father was kneeling down and holding his black beads, following along with the prayers as the radio priest said them, one after another.

The baby's name was Anne Laura, and we called her Nancy. Mimo said that was a nickname for Anne. Mimo and Daddy both made it clear that as much trouble as the baby was to me, I was stuck with her forever, at least until I grew up. She slept in a crib in Daddy's room, next to Mother and Daddy's big bed, and in the night when she cried for milk he got up and fixed her a bottle. Sometimes I would hear him walking around and I would get up, walk past my snoring Mimo who had taken out her false teeth and slept, her mouth open, in the bed across from mine.

—Back to bed, Mary Alice, Daddy always said. You need your beauty sleep.

—I want to feed the baby, too, I said.

—Not your job, he replied. My job, my duty. He walked back and forth across the room, patting the baby's back gently until she let out a big burp. I laughed and went back to bed.

After a time I stopped asking when my mother would be home. I figured she had gone to heaven to live with God the Father, but I couldn't remember who told me this. I knew it must have been one of the grownups.

The day was warm and sunny, and my father was in the kitchen fixing breakfast. The baby nurse had just arrived, in her stiff white uniform. Miss Jones was mean and strict, and she was interested only in the baby, and never me, except to scold me or correct my table manners. She was holding Nancy and cooing to her.

—There, there, little girl, settle down now.

—What time do you have to leave for the service? she asked my father.

Nine, he said. We'll be back by noon, at my mother's downstairs, for the reception after.

He helped me get ready. Mimo had taken me to the Tog Shop in Parkville to buy a new dress. Nothing too bright, she told Miss Elva, the clerk. She whispered something to Miss Elva, who looked surprised and then sad. She pulled three dresses from the rack and brought them to the dressing room.

—Which one do you like? Mimo asked me.

— I like them all, I told her.

I was afraid to ask why I needed a new dress anyway. New dresses were usually for birthday parties or Easter.

This one, then, Mimo said, holding up a blue jumper with a white blouse with ruffles on the cuffs. This goes well with your blue eyes. You're such a pretty little girl. She held out her arms and I climbed into her embrace. She hugged me for a long time, and her face was sad. A few tears ran down her cheeks.

—To think that I am burying my only child, she said softly.

—You don't have a child! I said.

—Honey, your mother was my child, she said quietly. Your father explained it all to you, didn't he?

I nodded.

—And he told you that your mother is in heaven now with the angels, didn't he?

I nodded again.

—And you understand that now, you have to be help to your father and to Nancy, don't you?

—I don't know how to help, I said.

—You help by being a good girl, Mimo said. And I know you will be. And when summer comes, Gene and I will come down in the Jeep and take you up to my house for the summer. Wouldn't that be nice?

I didn't answer.

—And you can feed Sheba the goat, and help me in the garden. Wouldn't you like that?

—Yes, maybe, I said.

Mimo told Miss Elva we would take the jumper and the ruffled blouse, and she told her to charge it to my mother's account.

She took the big brown box from Miss Elva.

—Come back soon and see us soon, Miss Elva said, smiling down at me through her thick glasses with the light brown edges.

Then, to Mimo, she said, I'm so sorry, Mrs. Shockney. What a tragedy.

We walked to the bus stop in silence.

Now the day had come, the special day at church, and I was the smallest one there. Everyone was a grownup except me: my aunts and uncles, my downstairs grandmother, Mimo, Dickie Ritz and Miss Emma, his wife, Miss Sophie and Mr. Wilbur from across the street, and my mother's friends from when she was a teacher, before I was born. I had been to Mass a few times with my father, but it was nothing like this. Instead of a church crowded with so many people that men had to stand in the aisles and in the back of the church, there was a small group of us in the front pews of the big church. My father sat between Mimo and me in the first pew, and my other grandmother and Aunt Sally next to me. The aunts and uncles were in the two rows behind us, and on the other side of the aisle, Mother's friends, all in dark coats and hats with black nets that came down part of the way over their eyes. They were all crying quietly, and dabbing at their eyes with white handkerchiefs.

The priest, his back to us, talked softly and I couldn't understand what he was saying. Then he stood on a tall platform with a wooden box in front of him and spoke about my mother, calling her Jean Marie. He said she had led a good life though it was cut short, and that she had now gone home to live with God forever. He talked on and on, and then turned his back to us again and talked very quietly, at one point holding up a white circle as the altar boy, wearing a black and white smock, rang a bell three times. Mimo held me on her lap while all the grownups went up to the front of the church, knelt down, and had communion. I wasn't old enough for that yet. I buried my face in Mimo's shoulder and inhaled the sweet smell of her coat. Her necklace rubbed against my forehead.

—I want to go home, I murmured.

—Soon, she said. Soon this will be over and we will all go to your other grandmother's for something to eat. You can go upstairs and get your doll if you want, before the reception.

One of the uncles, the one with no wife, drove us home in his shiny black car. I sat in the back and Mimo was in the front. Uncle Edgar turned on the radio. I heard the talking on the radio with a lot of strange noise in the background, and I tried to listen to what my uncle and Mimo were saying. Most of the words made no sense.

—Problems before the baby came, Mimo said. Headache, the doctors couldn't figure it out. Tried to stop it but it was too far gone.

Uncle Edgar didn't say much. Occasionally he would come out with one or two words in his deep voice.

—I see, he said. —Ain't that a shame, though.

Mimo was speaking very softly, and I knew she didn't want me to hear.

—They think she had a stroke, she said, and so young, too. I never heard of such a thing.

Stroke, that's the word I heard over and over again all afternoon, said in low tones, or whispered. The small living room of my downstairs grandmother's house was filled with people sitting, standing, and perched on the arms of the stuffed chairs or the sofa. They crowded onto the small front porch and smoked, or wandered from the dining room into the kitchen and to the sunporch. Whenever I moved near to one of the ladies who sat balancing a plate of chicken sandwiches, corn fritters and Waldorf salad on her lap, she would smile at me and say, what a pretty dress you're wearing, Mary Alice, or what a nice dolly you have. What's her name?

Soon coffee and cake were brought from the kitchen, a black walnut cake with hard white sugar icing that I liked to separate from the cake and eat like candy. Usually my mother or Aunt Sally scolded me for this, telling me eat the cake, too, or next time you'll get a plate of icing, no cake. But the cake was dry and I didn't like the walnuts with their strong taste and the black skins that stuck to my teeth. This day I wasn't interested in the icing. I found Mimo sitting in the kitchen in the corner, drinking coffee with so much cream that it looked more like cream with coffee in it than the other way around. She was picking at her cake and talking to Aunt Sally.

—I'll be back down to stay for a few days every few months, she said, and then in June, when the weather is nicer, I can take her up to Hersensburg for the summer. The mountain air will be good for her, and I can teach her how to plant a garden and feed the chickens. I climbed up on the red chair beside her, a chair that Aunt Sally said my father used to sit in when he was little, not yet tall enough to reach the dinner table. Aunt Sally and my father called it the Monkey Ward chair. I asked Aunt Sally about stroke.

She was stirring her coffee to cool it down. She looked up abruptly.

—Who told you that word? she asked.

—I just heard it a couple times, I said. In there. I pointed to the living room.

—Does it mean struck? I asked her.

—Yes, in a way it does. It means that the blood rushes up into the person's brain and sometimes there is something so wrong that they go to sleep and never wake up again.

—Like Mommy? I asked

—Yes, she said. I could see tears starting in her eyes and she took off her glasses and wiped her eyes with the back of her hand, the one that wasn't stirring the coffee.

—Mary Alice, let's go outside for a little swing, she said. She held out her hand to me. Her nails were short and pink. I didn't want to, but I took her hand and followed her outside. I climbed on the swing and she pushed me higher, higher, until I could see the top of the sunporch and the twigs and leaves stuck there on the green roof.

Then I was tired, and it was time for my nap. Aunt Sally took me upstairs to my bedroom and covered me with the old quilt Mimo had brought from Cumberland a long time ago. Aunt Sally sat on the edge of the bed while I closed my eyes. She stroked my forehead with her soft hand. I heard the voices from downstairs growing fainter.

Take Gutman

Elizabeth Gutman seemed extraordinarily powerful, both in intellect and in her clear resonant voice as she lectured on *The Golden Bowl* in a crowded, overheated third floor classroom. In those days, we would smoke in class, and the Marlboro and Gaulois clouds drifted up to the high ceiling as we watched her and simultaneously scribbled into our spiral notebooks. But physically, Mrs. Gutman appeared quite fragile. She wore no makeup. In winter, she dressed in two well-worn cardigans and a long wool coat. Her long blond hair was untamed and frizzy, forming a halo mass around her small face. Her eyes were a deep blue. She was the first professor who came to know me by name.

I had transferred from a small college, where I'd been a commuter, living at home in my family's three-decker in the Dorchester section of Boston. Coming to this elite school, I expected a more serious, all-consuming intellectual life, something absent from my first college. I hoped to meet professors who would challenge and inspire me, not merely march me and my classmates through midterms, papers and finals. But I had no idea how hard it would be to find housing on campus. I lived for several weeks in a dingy SRO hotel on the corner of Amsterdam and 121st, occupied by some very old women. A small group of us, all transfer students, shared the dismal suites of cramped bedrooms, 1920's-era bathrooms, and dark, ancient kitchens with some of these lonely old ladies.

It took me forever to find friends. And there seemed no quick way to make connections with my teachers, either in or out of class. On the corner across from the college gate, every afternoon and evening, a tall, skinny guy stood with his hand out, asking for spare change for a sandwich. I got into the habit of crossing the street a block earlier than I might have, just to avoid him. Almost every day, I saw the woman who appeared to be speaking in tongues yelling into the receiver of a broken payphone in front of the Campus Deli. The subway roared by the campus, day and night.

It was widely believed in my family that I had gotten above my raising, that the local Catholic girls' college back in Boston was perfectly fine for me and my cousins. When I set out for New York, I expected to find a welcoming community of sisters and teachers who would show us how to live the intellectual life. Instead, I was surrounded by those whose experiences I could only vaguely comprehend. At orientation, a girl with long red hair and ginger-colored eyes lit a cigarette, exhaled slowly and began, "As I was playing chess with an architect friend of mine last weekend—." The housing director was impervious to my frequent visits and polite requests for a room in the dorms. Had one opened up yet? There was never a hint of a smile from her. Eventually she stopped responding except with a shake of her head whenever I appeared in the doorway of her office.

"Take Gutman," said my orientation guide, a breezy, self-confident sophomore who enthusiastically gave me registration advice. "Gutman's amazing. She makes even Proust comprehensible."

A buzz spread among the transfer students. "I hear Gutman's really good."

"What does she teach?" I asked. I had no intention of majoring in English. I had been baptized in the waters of politics when I volunteered the previous summer for a senatorial candidate in my home state. He had won handily. I wanted to study political science, and anything standing in the way of that was a small hurdle I was ready to leap over.

"Who cares?" said another transfer, who came from a rich girls' junior college near Washington, DC. "If people say she's good, take her. I've had it with bad teachers, man."

What I didn't realize until I got to the first meeting of a class in the Modern Novel was that Gutman's classes were always full to overflowing. But she never turned anyone away. Guys from the men's college across the road routinely showed up to take her courses for credit, instead of auditing only for the purpose of meeting girls. Gutman didn't care how many students she had; she just kept adding small discussion sections on top of her lectures.

I'd never heard anyone lecture about novels before. I found Gutman's classes inspiring, stimulating, sometimes thrilling. Each ninety-minute class sped along as she spoke. I was enveloped in her outpouring of facts, literary theories, and intriguing connections between writers and texts. It was in one of those small discussion groups, as we worked our way through Proust (in French, for those who could read it), Mann (for those who knew German), Joyce and Faulkner that I was first able to speak out in class, to find a way out of my reserve and my feeling that I wasn't smart enough to contribute to the discussion.

Early in the term I handed in a paper, leaving it in Gutman's mailbox with a note attached, saying how grateful I was that she'd created the smaller sections where I felt comfortable enough to raise my hand. She returned the paper with many comments and probing questions, as always. But this time, she added an encouraging note. She said my ideas were "worth bringing to our class." I wasn't sure exactly what she meant, but I took it as a compliment.

I saw her on Wednesday afternoon teas, too, with her two blond children, a girl with thick braids, a boy all explosive energy, and I delighted in her greeting me—by name—with a wide smile and sparkling eyes. I have forgotten by now, all these years later, what I wrote my papers on, but I recall studying for the exam and relishing all I had learned about the roots of the modern novel, psychoanalytic theory, the New Criticism. Gutman had opened my mind up to all this. There was so much more to learn. I had no interest any longer in political science or history. I would major in English. I would ask Gutman to be my advisor. She would teach me everything she knew. I would model my intellectual life after hers.

After finals, I went home for the summer and waited tables at a fancy restaurant on the south shore. I stayed out late with my high school friends, drinking beer at the park and going down to the Cape if someone had extra room in the family cottage. I'd made some new friends at college, mostly a tight little group of girls who lived on my floor and had welcomed me into their camaraderie. One of them stayed on in New York for the summer, sharing an apartment on Riverside with grad students. One day a letter from her arrived, with a clipping from the university paper, summer edition.

Gutman was dead.

Lee had heard a story, one she didn't entirely believe. Gutman was preparing for a family vacation. She packed two enormous leather suitcases, and when she picked both of them up at the same time, she suffered a massive heart attack and died instantly. There were few details in the campus newspaper obituary, only a photo of her, that untidy curly hair, and an intense, direct look in her eyes. I am so sorry, Lee wrote. She knew how much I admired Gutman and was counting on her. I wondered who would push me, steer me, encourage me now. And I could not figure out why the circumstances of Gutman's death were a secret.

The summer passed in a blur of tables tended to, wine poured for customers, empty plates cleared, busy nights, dead-slow nights. On one particularly quiet evening the young assistant manager closed up early and let the help stay to have a little party. In the kitchen, we drank beer. One of the younger waitresses brought out her guitar and sang folk songs. A busser, a black kid from Roxbury, sang a Smokey Robinson song none of us had even gotten used to yet, it was so new, and we were so busy working that we had little time for the radio. The boy, no more than fifteen, rendered the tune smoothly, lyrically. White and black teenagers and adults stood around the kitchen swaying, feeling soulful. It was easy at moments like this not to think about Gutman. I stopped myself from wondering what had really gone on in her apartment that day. I could put it behind me.

And for a long time, I succeeded. I returned to New York in the fall. I found a new advisor, a brusque middle-aged spinster who wore tweed suits and sensible shoes and didn't care what courses I took so long as I satisfied all my major requirements. Several summers later—by that time I had married and, finding myself very unhappy I was already separated and on my way to a divorce—I went up north to a writers' conference. By now, I fancied myself a poet.

One of the writers there had known Gutman in New York. I had come to work on my poetry, but to tell the truth, I didn't get much done. Instead, I found every opportunity to talk to the poet alone, to ask him about Gutman. I learned in minute increments, over several days talking with the grizzled fellow, that the circumstances of Gutman's life were very sad—no, tragic, like the stuff of the novels we studied in her course that winter. She had taken her own life. I didn't have the nerve to ask for the gruesome details, whether her husband had found her, who had raised their children. I didn't even know how to phrase the questions. I just sank back into my Adirondack chair, looking down at the grass. I felt such surprise; my face flushed hot. What had there been that I had not seen? What insights had eluded me, when the evidence had been right there before me?

Whatever sadness and pain there had been in Gutman's life, I had been oblivious, dense. She should have become a gifted teacher who lived on to teach until old age came to her. The best I can say, which isn't very much at all from where I stand now, is that she'd made her mark on me. It all seems so distant now, those afternoons in Vermont, as I tried to tease facts from a man I hardly knew, about a woman I felt I had known so well. I took as much as I could from Gutman, but it could never be enough for me.

Good Catholics

I knew my father would never let me go on a blind date with one of Betts' football friends. I could just hear him saying, *You're only fourteen. What do I know about this boy? You haven't even met him? You're too young to go out with a sixteen- year-old.* In the end, I backed out of Betts' scheme to fix me up with a second-string fullback from St. Ignatius. When I told her that blind date was off, I felt strangely relieved, as though I was never the slightest bit interested in the first place. I preferred to stay home while everyone else was twisting the night away—that is, if we had been allowed to do the twist at Our Lady of Good Counsel dances.

I was stuck on the sidelines, watching the pre-dance frenzy take place everywhere—on the city bus to or from school, before homeroom, in the cafeteria, even in those briefly scribbled notes girls wrote on small corners of paper, torn out of history or English notes and passed across the aisle while the nun's back was turned. What will you wear? What sort of jewelry? What color shoes? Where did you buy your dress? Is your mother making your dress? Is it a Vogue pattern or a Simplicity? I found myself tuning out whenever I could, opening the algebra book in the mornings before the homeroom bell and pretending to be absorbed in working out a proof, or eating lunch quickly and waiting for class in the empty classroom, reading a magazine or reviewing my homework.

I never expected Kate to take up the project of finding me a date, a project that I privately began to think of as Mary Alice's First Date. Kate hatched a plan. She had some boy cousins, the McKees, five of them. One was our age, and another, two years older. Mike had his driver's license. Patrick and Kate, who were the same age, had been playmates since they were babies. It was the perfect solution, said Kate. —You go with Mike and we can double date.

—It'll be great, she said. She was carefully unwrapping a peanut butter and jelly sandwich, the same thing she brought for lunch very day. I pulled my frugal lunch out of the brown paper sack, two hard boiled eggs and a bag of celery and carrot sticks.

—Mike can drive us. Your father will like them, they're really nice guys.

I nodded. I figured my father wouldn't mind my going out with Kate and her cousins.

—Do they dance? I asked her.

Kate looked at me skeptically. —What do you mean? Of course they dance, she said. D'you think they're from Mars?

—I mean, are they good dancers?

—Sure, she said. —They're fine. And they're really funny. You'll like them, especially Mike.

By that Friday, Mike had phoned me to formally accept my invitation to the dance, which Kate had conveyed to him. He had a pleasant, deep voice, and an easy laugh. I didn't feel at all nervous about the date, the dance, or what I anticipated would be my father's awkward and brief interrogation of Mike when he came to pick me up. My father didn't object to the plan, because he had met Kate's parents and thought they were good Catholics.

Kate and I went dress shopping. We coordinated our outfits, making sure that we weren't going to look like twins. She chose a pink satin dress with a full gathered skirt. It made her waist look tiny, as if she were a little doll. I settled on a blue velveteen suit-dress. I loved the round Chanel collar, which looked like something out of a fashion magazine. The skirt was narrow, the lines straight and clean. When I put it on, I felt like a sophisticated New Yorker.

On the afternoon of the dance I filed and polished my nails, did some homework, took a long bath, and then carefully laid out my clothes on the bed. My little sister came in and chattered away as I arranged everything—underwear, garter belt, brand new nylon stockings still in their fancy cardboard box, bra, slip, imitation pearls, shoes. The two-piece velveteen suit was hanging in the department store bag in the closet. I had clipped off the price tags but had otherwise not touched it, fearing it might be bad luck to do so until now.

—Can I touch it? Nancy asked. —My hands are clean, See? She held them out, palms up, for my inspection.

—Sure. But go with the grain, like this. I demonstrated. The material felt soft and thick.

—It's beautiful, Nancy said. —Hurry up, put it on. You are going to look like a princess.

I shooed her out of the room and slowly began to get dressed. Before I stepped into the dress, I did my makeup—just lipstick and a little powder. Then I pulled on the skirt. I loved the feel of the silky lining as it brushed against my ankles. I drew it up until the waistband sat where it should, and buttoned and zipped the skirt closed. It felt just right, even better than the day I had tried it on in the store. Next came the top, a sort of jacket, but one that needed no blouse underneath it. I fastened each imitation pearl button slowly, then stood back and looked in the mirror. I thought I looked pretty good.

Mike arrived at quarter to eight on the dot, just as he had promised. My father answered the front door, then the two of them came upstairs to our apartment and sat in the living room. I pretended I wasn't yet ready, even though I had been dressed for at least an hour. I heard them clearly, two deep voices. My father asked Mike about his school, and Mike responded with long answers, as if they had known each other forever. It was time to make my entrance. All I lacked was a staircase to float down, but since this was an apartment, that wasn't possible. Oh, well, I thought, that only happens on television.

Mike was tall, red-haired and freckled all over—at least his face, neck and hands, which was all I could see of his skin. He had blue eyes and straight teeth. He wasn't really handsome, but he wasn't bad-looking. I smiled and then didn't know what to do next.

My father said, Mike here tells me he plays lacrosse.

—Yes sir, in the spring, Mike said. He was sitting on the sofa, one arm across the back of it. His long legs were extended and crossed at the ankle. I noticed his shiny black shoes.

—That was an Indian sport, my father said. —The Indians taught it to white men.

—Yes, sir, they did, Mike said.

My father abruptly said, Mike, I want you to have Mary Alice home by no later than eleven-thirty.

—Yes sir, Mike said. And we were off, down the stairs and out the front door. A beat-up station wagon was parked in front of the house. I tried not to make a face.

—It's not as bad on the inside, Mike said. He opened the front passenger door for me. I slid into the seat, happy that the weather was chilly enough that I had to wear a coat. The inside of the car smelled like stale cigarette smoke, and I didn't want to get anything on my new dress, which had cost more than any single outfit I had had in my life up till then.

Kate and Patrick sat in the back seat, laughing. She introduced me to him, and they resumed their private conversation. I felt nervous, not knowing how to chat with my date. Mike must have felt the same, because he switched on the radio. He kept time to the music by tapping his fingers on the steering wheel. The ride to Our Lady wasn't long, so we were spared too many long, awkward silences.

I wasn't prepared for the way the cafeteria had been transformed. It looked like a real dance floor, with an elevated platform across one long wall for the band, and streamers in twisted ribbons hanging from the ceilings. The everyday fluorescent lights in the ceiling were turned off, and standing lamps in the corners and along the walls provided a soft golden light. Some tables had been moved out, and the rest were pushed up against the wall around the periphery of the cafeteria. The tables were covered with paper tablecloths, and decorated with small vases of flowers.

—Wow, Kate said.

—Pretty cool, Mike said. Since we were early, we got a choice table not far from the bandstand. The sound system played records as the band set up. Milling around the bandstand were four teenaged boys, three with guitar cases and one who set up a drum kit. A fifth boy was lugging a large amplifier. He set it down in the corner of the wooden platform, then he seemed to follow directions from one of the guitar players.

The room began to fill up as though a bus had pulled up in the parking lot to disgorge twenty or thirty couples. Chaperones, a few mothers and one father, stood near the cafeteria kitchen door, paying no attention to us, chatting among themselves. They were setting up a long table with punch bowls, paper cups, and bowls of pretzels and potato chips. Mike patted his jacket pocket and drew out a pack of cigarettes.

—Not inside, dear, said one of the mothers. She pointed to the Exit sign. Mike rolled his eyes.

—You smoke? He asked me. I shook my head.

—I'm dying for one, he said. —I'll just step outside. Want to come with me?

Kate interrupted him. —Mary Alice and I are going to the ladies' room, she said, giving him a stern look. —We'll meet you guys back here in five minutes. Pat volunteered to save our seats.

Things were not off to a good start. Kate and I stood side by side in the girls room, checking our hair and out lipstick. She told me things would be fine one the music started.

—Mike's a great dancer, she said.

She was right about that. I would rather have danced to records, but the band seemed to know enough new songs, and they played loud and fast most of the time, with a slow dance thrown in now and then. Mike was energetic, a showoff. People near him seemed to lose track of what they were doing and stare at him as he twisted, turned, jumped, wiggled, all in time to the beat, and with athletic energy. All I had to do was imitate his steps and try to keep up. The slow dances were more of a problem for me. He started out with his right arm on my waist and his left clasping my right hand politely, with a few inches between our chests, but as the song wore on, he pulled me closer, and pushed our clasped hands over his heart. I'd seen couples do this, but they were the ones who'd been going steady for a long time. I pulled away a little, and tried to talk about the music, but it was so loud Mike couldn't hear what I was saying, or he pretended he couldn't.

By the end of the evening I wanted only to go home. Mike had left the dance three times for smoke breaks, and I found the smell of cigarette smoke sickening. Kate had to be home earlier than me, so she and Pat asked to be dropped off first.

Mike and I rode in silence. This time, he didn't even turn on the radio. Four blocks from school, he turned left, onto a road that passed through the public golf course.

—This isn't the right way, I told him.

—I know, he said. I just thought we'd stop here for a bit and talk, you know. He pulled off the road into a small wooded area, turned off the ignition switch and the headlights. There was no moon. He slid his arm along the seat behind me and pulled me toward him.

I didn't know what to do. I turned to say something to him and he came in for a kiss. I remember thinking, a kiss is okay, it's about time I was kissed. But then I felt his tongue pushing between my lips and his arm drawing me towards him. He pressed me towards him, and with his other hand, he worked his way down the front of my dress and into the top of my bra.

—Stop it! I said. —Stop. I pushed his hand away from my chest.

—Take me home. Now.

—M.A. come on, he said. Don't be like that.

I folded my arms tightly and shifted away from him and closer to the passenger door.

—Take me home now or I will scream, I said. I worried that nobody was around to hear me on that empty golf course.

My face felt hot. I bit my lip so I wouldn't start crying, the last thing in the world I wanted to do.

Mike removed his arm from the back of the seat and sat back behind the wheel. He felt for his cigarettes and turned the key in the ignition, then lit his cigarette from the car's lighter.

—Have it your way, he said in a strange, gruff voice. He inhaled and blew out a long puff of smoke. Then he backed the car up quickly and pulled onto the golf course dirt road, onto the parkway that led to my neighborhood.

When we reached my house, I was furious. —Don't bother to turn off the car.

I jerked open the door, jumped out, and slammed the car door as hard as I could.

Mike leaned over and would down the passenger side window.

—You think you're so cool, don't you? He called after me, Stuck up, that's what you are. Stuck up and frigid!

I didn't turn around. My heart was pounding. I just hoped my father wasn't waiting up for me. The front door was unlocked just as Dad had told me it would be. I opened it, slipped inside, and leaned against it with all my weight to shut it tight. I turned the double lock and heard it click into place. Mike's car started, then the engine noise faded as he drove off.

I stayed leaning against the heavy front door, listening for any sounds from our apartment upstairs. Nothing. I clicked on the light, made my way up the stairs, then carefully opened the door at the top. I shut off the light over the staircase. I could see a nightlight on in the hall, like always. I slipped off my high heels and carried them, tiptoed to my bedroom, and undressed in the dark, leaving my underwear in a pile near the foot of the bed. I laid my dress across the straight-backed chair in the corner. My nightgown was where I had left it that morning, neatly folded and tucked under my pillow, so I felt for it in the dark and pulled it over my head.

Nancy was in a deep sleep, curled up with her teddy bear next to her. She was holding it by the leg, and most of the bear was draped over the edge of the bed. I pushed it back gently, and she stirred slightly, then turned over onto her stomach, her face buried in the pillow.

I was about to climb into bed when I remembered that I hadn't brushed my teeth. I thought again of Mike's tongue pushing into my mouth, and quickly shut out that thought. I tiptoed into the bathroom and brushed my teeth quietly, using as little water as I could, so as not to awaken my father. I splashed water on my face, patted it dry, and went back to my room.

I slipped into bed, pulled the quilt up snug under my chin and turned towards the wall. I could never tell a soul what had happened. As of that moment, I didn't care if I ever went out on another date. I tried to think about how everything had begun so well—Kate's plan, her wish to include me, her sweet generosity. That was on one side of the ledger, and on the other, there was her wolf of a cousin, Mike—obnoxious, forward, and unrepentant.

Sleep would not come quickly this night, I knew. I listened to Nancy's quiet breathing. I shut my eyes and saw necklaces of shapes, at first in black and white, then as my breathing slowed down at last, the beads began to be saturated with color, pink at first, then rose and purple. I lay there listening to the familiar nighttime noises, the creak of wood, the sound of a car, the man up the street who worked nights, perhaps, or someone driving on Harford Road. For a long time, I resisted sleep, watching images that weren't quite dreams but weren't real, either.

Tomorrow was Sunday, early Mass, and afterwards, we'd stop for sweet rolls from the bakery as we did each week. I felt like a junior grade Saint Maria Goretti, though that seemed far-fetched. I didn't have fourteen stab wounds, including a fatal one to the heart, only hurt pride and annoyance. I didn't particularly feel that I had staved off mortal sin, anything like that. I didn't feel happy about pushing Mike away, but he had asked for it. He had tried to go from zero miles an hour to a hundred in one evening, without really knowing who I was, or caring to know.

I was really looking forward to the sweet rolls.

Fusion

Claire was stuck in traffic, edging into the left turn lane just before Central Square, when she glanced over to a side street and saw the makeshift booth set up. Someone had used black magic marker to draw a Hitler mustache on the president's face. She used to love that campaign poster, the one that proclaimed HOPE in large letters across the bottom.

It was those kids again, the ones who sold the newspaper with the same bizarre fake news stories every month. The car ahead of her wasn't moving an inch, and Claire leaned to her left to find out what was causing the holdup. A long line of cars stood idling in the left lane. Maybe the signal was on the fritz. Or someone wanting to make a left turn was waiting for a break. Either way, Claire had time to observe the action on the sidewalk. IMPEACH HIM!, the poster's block letters entreated passers-by. Two women with young children veered away from the kids in the booth, moving into the crosswalk to cross Mass Ave.

Claire was on her way to visit her friend Rosie, who was at home recovering from surgery. Claire had promised Rosie she'd be over by one. It was nearly two, and Claire still faced a good half hour more in heavy traffic. That did not deter her from making a detour, a hasty left turn a few blocks off the road to Rosie's. She felt lucky to find a parking space near the booth the kids had set up. She fished in her handbag for quarters for the parking meter, but came up empty. I'll take a chance, she thought, I'll only be a few minutes. She jammed her handbag under the front seat where no thieves would notice it. Rosie's car had recently been broken into at a gas station when she went inside to pay the cashier. The insurance claims man told her she should never leave anything in sight in the car, especially in a locked car.

"Not even a coffee cup," he said. Rosie reported this to Claire, who took it to heart. Sometimes she cheated a bit, leaving a neatly folded Whole Foods bag on the passenger side floor in front. But the last thing Claire wanted was a busted window, glass everywhere, her wallet gone. She used her foot to maneuver the handbag until all of it, even the straps, disappeared under the driver's seat.

She clicked the key lock, which made a satisfying beep. She eyed the poster. The Hitler mustache really got on her nerves. When she was within fifteen feet of the kids hectoring people who passed by, she stopped. Which one should she approach first, she wondered. What should she say?

A pale woman with long brown hair pulled back with a plastic headband, looking every bit like a young suburban mother in her summer skirt and sandals, thrust a piece of paper in Claire's face. Claire took a couple steps back. The young woman moved towards her and was now as close as a longtime confidante at a funeral. Claire got a whiff of what she thought was soap, or maybe shampoo. She stepped back again, to give herself room to breathe.

The young woman began to speak, and continued for a few minutes without taking a breath. This was a prepared lecture, about Obama shutting down all the nuclear reactors and taking us all back to medieval times, something about the Knights of Rhodes, hospices for the dying that were really euthanasia operations, and a cover-up related to the murder of Muammar Khadafi. Claire felt dizzy. When the young woman stopped to take a breath, Claire saw her opening.

"Look, I'm not interested in what you're selling—"

"We're not selling anything," the young woman said. Claire now thought of her as a girl, because in truth, she was much younger than Claire had thought at first. "Unless you'd like to buy one—" She thrust a pamphlet at Claire, who kept her arms folded tightly across her chest.

Claire shook her head and made a face the one her ex-husband liked to tease her about—her disgusted expression, he had called it, like she'd just smelled something foul.

"Just a second, I want to ask you something," Claire said. She looked directly into the girl's very green eyes. "When was the last time you called your parents?"

The girl ignored her and talked about impeachment and the necessity of avoiding a third world war.

"Really, when was the last time?" Claire continued. "Your mother hasn't heard from you in months. She's worried. When was the last time you called her?"

The girl tried again to deliver her speech. She shrugged and returned to the booth. She called out to a couple of women who were passing by. They were speaking Spanish and holding two little boys by the hand. Neither of them paid any attention to her.

Claire looked at the others working with the long-haired girl. One was a young man with a short, tidy haircut. He wore a white shirt tucked into belted khaki pants. Claire thought he looked like a Mormon missionary, or a Jehovah's Witness, except that he wasn't wearing a tie. Two women stayed behind the booth, organizing flyers and trying to keep them from blowing away in the breeze.

"Our First Amendment at work," Claire said aloud. Then she looked around to be sure nobody had heard her. She walked back to her car, clicked the electronic key, and when the car chirped, she climbed inside the car. She dislodged her handbag from under the driver's seat and tossed it onto the front passenger seat. She popped in a mix CD her son had made for her. On the outside of the silver disc, he had written a label in his cramped hand, Folk Oldies. The first song was a Simon and Garfunkel, and it was a wonder her twenty-year-old son knew this one. "Let us be lovers, we'll marry our fortunes together," sang the youthful voices. She enjoyed the sad feeling listening to the song gave her. It reminded her of college. She had loved lying back on her bed in the dorm, closing her eyes and listening to the same record for hours on end.

She glanced over at the sidewalk activists. What she had really wanted to say to the girl was, *I know what will become of you if you don't leave this business now. If you would just call your mother, that would be a start.*

Claire knew all about this group, almost back to its beginnings, years earlier. She had a friend from high school days, a girl from the northwest side of town. Helaine was the only child of a Swedish father and an American mother. The athletic activities at their all-girls Catholic school were limited to basketball, field hockey, and lacrosse. Helaine was a golfer, and a very good one. She competed in tournaments and racked up many prizes. Claire watched as Helaine not only made first honors every quarter, but also achieved a name for herself in the small world of high school women's golf. When it came time to apply to college, Claire and her friends applied to state universities, but Helaine went to an elite women's college, in the days before the Ivy League schools went co-ed.

She visited Helaine often, driving up to Pennsylvania to spend the weekend. Her friend had mastered the art of irony early on, and could bring down anyone—a snobby girl, a boy with bad manners, or a full-of-himself assistant professor—with a succinct, understated observation.

"You might want to reconsider that heinous jacket," Claire once saw Helaine say to a rich girl from New York whose mother had been a daytime TV star. "Wearing fur is tantamount to asking to have paint splattered on you," Helaine continued. The girl looked shocked. Then she walked straight back to her dorm room to change her coat.

Claire and Helaine stayed up late discussing Sartre and Camus. They leafed through *Vogue* and *Harper's Bazaar* to take note of the season's fashions. Sometimes they rode the commuter train into Philly, looking for sale bargains at

Wanamaker's or Bonita Teller. They went to mixers at the men's college nearby, smoked grass and danced in a big circle with the stoners. Helaine majored in philosophy and went to Sunday Mass. Claire lived at home and went to a local state college. She majored in education and became an agnostic, sleeping in on Sunday mornings.

Then Helaine met a boy, someone she thought Claire should meet. She asked Claire to come up, she wanted to introduce Claire to him. Claire didn't see what the big deal was. The guy wasn't much of a student, though she had to admit that from the photo Helaine sent, the two of them sitting under a tree, he looked very cool in his work shirt, long hair and love beads.

Soon it seemed that Claire could never reach Helaine on the dorm phone and even if she left a message, Helaine never returned the calls. The amusing letters dropped off altogether. Claire met the new boyfriend briefly, when she was on her way to the train after a weekend visit with Helaine. He was handsome, blue-eyed, blond, and a few years older than Helaine and Claire. He offered Claire a joint for the road, but she declined. He didn't seem smart enough to be a philosophy major, but then, she'd never been in a class with him, so maybe she was missing something.

Claire didn't forget about Helaine, but she no longer wrote to her. It was too hard to do all the work of the friendship, and Helaine seemed to have time only for her studies and for her boyfriend. Months passed, and then a year or two. Things change, Claire thought, friendships wither.

Claire heard from the old high school grapevine that Helaine had a new love interest. She had asked their mutual classmates about Claire, what she was doing, whether she had gotten married yet. Of course, thought Claire, it was just like Helaine to find another boyfriend immediately after dumping the old one. This one had graduated and moved to California, where he was getting a master's in chemistry. He was also dealing drugs, mostly acid—which it was said he cooked up in his lab—and he flew Helaine out to visit him every month. Claire didn't think this was such a great idea, but who was she to say? She and her college dropout boyfriend were moving in together, despite her parents' disapproval. She didn't have a job lined up, and he hadn't finished school. They slept on a double mattress on the floor, and the rest of their possessions consisted of books and records, a chest of drawers they found on the curb on campus move out day, unmatched hand-me-down china from his mother, and forks and spoons they pilfered from the dorm cafeterias.

All this seemed to meet the definition of news, so Claire decided to write to her old friend. Helaine wrote back that she'd broken off with her drug dealer and decided to stay in Philadelphia for grad school. She was sharing an apartment with three other girls. "Right near the art museum, you should come up and visit," Helaine wrote.

Claire called Helaine. "I'll take a raincheck. I can't come just now. Maybe in June after school lets out, when I have more time."

Helaine sounded annoyed. "There's important work being done here," she said, "I'd love you to see what we're doing." Claire had no idea what the important work was.

Claire said, "Maybe after Christmas." When she hung up, she felt as though something had happened to Helaine, but she wasn't sure what that might be. She sounded so different. She hadn't cracked one joke, or asked Claire about her social life. There had been no mention of shopping for clothes, or new music that had caught Helaine's fancy.

On days when her seventh graders wrung every last ounce of energy from her, Claire's heart lifted when she sorted through the mail and saw the brown ink Helaine always used, and the good ivory stationery. Helaine was immersing herself in Wittgenstein, but not in school this time. She was working her way through it all on her own. She wrote about demonstrations by poor people whose rented homes were being bought up by the ever-expanding university, and the students who had joined her group's sit-ins. She was now part of a political faction that splintered off from the anti-university expansion group. Claire stuffed the letter into her top desk drawer, pushing it way in the back with store receipts and canceled checks.

Every few months Helaine called, inviting her to attend some conference or another, about welfare rights, or anti-war demonstrations. The first few times, Claire said she'd think about it, but she always ended up begging off. She tried to explain that she was overwhelmed by her teaching duties and needed the weekends to catch up on paperwork and tend to house chores.

But Claire missed Helaine, and after few more invitations, from her old friend, Claire told herself that it would be a short trip down to Washington, where Helaine had another one of her conferences. Claire figured she could take Helaine out for a meal, find out more about exactly what she was up to. They could have a little reunion, maybe a nice Italian supper with wine in Georgetown. She drove down on a rainy Saturday. Following Helaine's precise directions, she found the church parish hall, an old brown building in Northeast. A piece of white tagboard taped to the door pointed Claire to the welfare rights

conference in the basement. A battered coffee urn was set up on a metal table in the back of the hall. Styrofoam cups were laid out, with sugar and powdered creamer, which Claire hated. Speakers lectured about the conjunctive crisis in capitalism, a phrase that was repeated in the presentations all day long. The speakers alluded to mysterious conspiracies between Israel and the Queen of England. They insisted that there were connections between the Queen and international drug cartels. Claire's brain was spinning. She couldn't figure out whether Helaine's comrades were geniuses or whether they were brainwashed.

Helaine said she didn't have time to go out to dinner. She had to catch a ride back to Philly, where she said her colleagues were waiting for her.

"My God, you have to eat," Claire said. "Come have supper with me."

Again, Helaine refused. Claire dropped her off at a dilapidated frame house on a rundown block to meet her ride. All the way home, Claire felt confused. She wished she hadn't gone to Helaine's conference. She thought of all the things she could have done with those hours—make curtains for the kitchen, repot the plants that were rootbound, put in her monthly hours at the food co-op. Instead, she had listened to six hours of bullshit.

There were no more letters, no phone calls between the two women. Two or three years passed. Claire heard from the old high school grapevine that Helaine had dropped out of grad school. When Helaine's mother died, Claire's mother clipped the obituary from the *Post* and mailed it to her. Claire had an old phone number in Philadelphia for Helaine, so she called it, thinking she might get some ex-roommate of Helaine's who might provide a current number.

Helaine answered. Claire felt nervous. She expected Helaine to show some surprise at hearing from her.

Claire told Helaine she was sorry to hear about her mother's death.

"It wasn't a surprise," Helaine said, in a flat tone of voice. "She had cancer. She was sick a long time."

Claire asked, "How are you doing? Are you okay? Twenty-eight is young to lose a mother. I'm so sorry."

"It's fine, I'm fine," Helaine said. "Everything's okay. You really should come down and visit. We have a conference coming up. I've been doing some writing for Ralph." Ralph was the head of her political party, or whatever the group was. Claire waited for Helaine to stop talking. She couldn't make sense of what Helaine was saying. She stared at the flowered kitchen wallpaper and tried to think of a way to end the conversation.

"I have to go," Claire said, even though it wasn't true. "I have a meeting myself, in about an hour, and I'm taking the bus, it's a long ride."

She hung up and stared at the yellow receiver resting in its cradle. She thought of the many phones she had talked to Helaine on over the years, starting in high school with the old black rotary phone that sat on a side table in the living room, then the blue Princess phone her parents gave her for her sixteenth birthday, the hall phones in the college dorm, the avocado green kitchen phone her parents had when Claire lived at home. Now, this yellow wall phone stared back at her with its twelve touchtone button eyes. She was not going to go to any more of Helaine's conferences. She would not allow herself to be recruited.

A year later, Helaine called.

"I got married," she announced. Claire had a moment of elation, a flashing image of Helaine in a simple white dress, holding a bouquet of daisies.

"Who?" Claire asked. "Who is he?"

It didn't take long for Helaine to explain. Claire understood: he was another of those pale people from Helaine's cult.

Claire's mind wandered as Helaine rambled on about her work and her husband's role in the Movement. Instead of paying attention to Helaine's monolog, Claire recollected the time she bumped into a longhaired girl who had gone to college with Helaine. The guests sat on the floor and listened to Neil Young, while they drank red wine and passed around a joint.

"She used to be so religious," the girl said. "Never knew anyone so Catholic. Went to church every Sunday. Worse than an orthodox Jew—my grandmother's orthodox, believe me, I know from religious fanatics. Then she got that boyfriend, the one who went to California, and she threw over the religion, stopped going to church. When he dumped her, she took up something just as strict as being Catholic, I guess."

Claire thought the girl had a point.

Now, as Claire interrupted Helaine to ask details about the wedding, Helaine said she and Garth had a quick ceremony at city hall on a Monday morning. Someone from the clerk's office was the witness. They got married and went straight back to work.

"Playing any golf?" Claire asked, regretting that she'd asked as soon as the words were out of her mouth. Helaine said she had sold her clubs; she was too busy to play. She had important work to do, work that was going to change this country.

More time passed, this time several years. Helaine called again, as though there'd been no hiatus in their friendship. There was no catching up, none of their old gossiping. Helaine said the anti-nuke protesters at the New Hampshire power plant were out to destroy American society, bent on returning us to the cruel world of the Middle Ages. The real answer, Helaine went on, was fusion energy. Fusion was the future. Ralph, the Movement's leader, knew a lot about fusion. He had collaborated with some outstanding physicists to spread the gospel of fusion.

"Helaine, stop. Stop a moment," Claire said, interrupting her old friend. There was silence on the other end of the line.

Then Claire heard herself say, words she had practiced in her head for a long time, but never thought she'd be able to say. "Don't call me again. I'm hanging up now. Don't call me, ever."

She was shaking as she replaced the receiver into the phone's base softly, as though to spare Helaine. Her face felt hot.

One summer afternoon when they were still in high school, Helaine pulled up in front of Claire's home in a black Beetle convertible. She gave the horn three short toots. The car's top was down, and Helaine had pulled her golden hair into a ponytail. Her clubs, in a brown leather golf bag, lay across the back seat. Claire ran down the front steps of her house, carrying only her cigarettes. A five-dollar bill was tucked into the pocket of her shorts. Claire slid into the passenger seat while Helaine turned up the volume on the radio.

"Where to?" Claire asked her friend. Helaine laughed and shifted into first gear.

"Anywhere we want," Helaine said, and they were off, onto the parkway and down into the city.

Lynne Viti was born and raised in Baltimore, Maryland and now lives in Massachusetts. She is a senior lecturer emerita in the Writing Program at Wellesley College. She received her B.A. *cum laude* in English from Barnard College, and her M.A. in Teaching of English from Teachers College, Columbia University, and earned her Ph.D. and J.D. from Boston College, where she was a university fellow in English. Her doctoral dissertation focused on the novels of Henry James and George Eliot.

Upon graduating from law school, she clerked for the Justices of Superior Court of Massachusetts, and subsequently was Chief Law Clerk to the Justices. She served as an assistant general counsel at the Massachusetts Bay Transportation Authority, then as a litigation associate at the Boston law firm of Harrison and Maguire before she resumed her full-time teaching career at Wellesley College.

Viti has authored two poetry collections, *Baltimore Girls* (2017) and *The Glamorganshire Bible* (2018), both from Finishing Line Press, and three online poetry microchapbooks, published by the Origami Poems Project. Her poetry, nonfiction and fiction have appeared in over a hundred journals and anthologies, including *Welcome to the Neighborhood, The Wire: Urban Decay and American Television, Chautauqua Review, Constellations, The Somerville Times, Nixes Mate Review, Gargoyle, The Baltimore Sun, Amuse-Bouche,* and *The Paterson Review.* She was awarded Honorable Mentions in the 2018, 2019 and 2020 WOMR/Joe Gouveia Outermost Poetry Contests, the 2015 Allen Ginsberg Poetry Contest, and won the summer 2015 poetry contest at *The Song Is.* Her short story, "Tony Bennett, Aldous Huxley, and Eddie" was awarded an Honorable Mention in the 2015 Glimmer Train Short Fiction Contest. She blogs at lynneviti.wordpress.com.

www.ingramcontent.com/pod-product-compliance
Lightning Source LLC
Chambersburg PA
CBHW030107040726
47494CB00025B/2214